the problem with paradise

LESLEY DAHL

the problem with paradise

delacorte press

Published by Delacorte Press
an imprint of Random House Children's Books
a division of Random House, Inc.
New York

www.randomhouse.com/kids

Educators and librarians, for a variety of teaching tools,
visit us at www.randomhouse.com/teachers

Library of Congress Cataloging-in-Publication Data
Dahl, Lesley.
The problem with paradise / Lesley Dahl.
p.   cm.
Summary: Fourteen-year-old Casey dreads leaving her friends and boyfriend
to spend a boring summer on a Caribbean island with her naturalist father,
stepmother, and brothers, but she has some life-changing experiences
that include learning to sail, helping with turtle conservation,
surviving storms, and romance.
ISBN-10: 0-385-73335-6 (trade hardcover)—
ISBN-10: 0-385-90352-9 (Gibraltar lib. bdg.)
ISBN-13: 978-0-385-73335-9 (trade hardcover)—
ISBN-13: 978-0-385-90352-3 (Gibraltar lib. bdg.)
[1. Coming of age—Fiction. 2. Wildlife conservation—Fiction.
3. Turtles—Fiction. 4. Vacations—Fiction. 5. Hurricanes—
Fiction. 6. West Indies—Fiction.] I. Title.
PZ7.D15118Pro 2006
[Fic]—dc22   2006004570

The text of this book is set in 12-point Goudy.

Book design by Kenneth Holcomb

Printed in the United States of America

10 9 8 7 6 5 4 3 2 1

First Edition

For Tom, who makes everything possible

Endless gratitude to Merrill Joan Gerber, for her friendship and example, for never tiring of telling me what I can do, and for never wanting to waste even five precious minutes on small talk.

More thanks than I can express to my friend, Cathie Sandstrom Smith, for her limitless love and encouragement.

I am blessed to have as friends Marta Carlson, Sharon Goldstein, Maria Impala and Patty O'Connor. Thank you for your never-ending support, reading and rereading, and for years of laughter and conversation. Many thanks go to Karol Ballard for her outstanding sense of humor and tireless cheerleading.

To my agent at ICM, Tina Dubois Wexler, thank you, *thank you*. I don't know how I got so lucky—you are a dream.

I was very fortunate to have Stephanie Lane at Delacorte Press take this book on, and I am grateful to her for making it better, and for being so easy to work with.

Many thanks to my early readers for their insightful and encouraging comments: Ayami Hiroshige, Alexis Summit, Emily Summit and Taylor Testa.

Tom Hill—my thanks go on forever.

For the first time ever I'm dying for class to start. Not because I'm wild about American government, believe me. The guy who teaches it, Mr. Halverson, should have done us all a patriotic favor and retired about the time the ink was drying on his beloved Constitution. I'm desperate to talk to Jen, my best friend. I have the worst news. I just found out last night, thanks to Mom's plans for me and my brothers, that my whole summer is ruined. I feel completely helpless, like I have no say whatsoever in how *my* life gets lived.

I really need to talk to Jen. I texted her all through homeroom, trying to get her to meet me in the bathroom before class, or at least to show up early for a change. No luck. She must not have been able to look at her cell phone, or worse, it was confiscated. That's what Halverson would do to mine now if he saw me checking it every three seconds. All I can do is wait, eyes glued to the hall door.

If I know Jen, she'll waltz into class the very instant the

bell rings. Before the bell *stops* ringing she'll be in her seat, hands folded, smiling. This keeps teachers with the "in your seat" rule from getting to mark her tardy, even though they know she's purposely pushing the being on time thing to a technicality.

The bell rings. Sure enough, Jen strolls in. She crosses right in front of Halverson to get to her desk in the last row, four over from me. The whole way, as if she's got all the time in the world, she's gathering her blond hair up into one of those twisted knots she's so good at. She's the first one on the attendance sheet: Jennifer Abbot. Just as her butt is coming in for a landing, she piles her hair on top of her head, clips it into place and calls out "Here" before old Halverson finishes calling her name. It makes him nuts. Of course, I've been in my seat for five minutes, and as soon as he's called my name, twenty-fourth on the list—Casey Stern—I give Jen the "check your cell" sign, tap-tap-tapping my own, which I have hidden in the palm of my hand. She shakes her head, air-slices her throat and sticks out her tongue in the "dead battery" sign. Fine, we'll have to do this the old-fashioned way. Using my hands under my desk, I give Jen the Signal.

Jen rolls her eyes. I glare hard at her and jerk my head in Halverson's direction.

"Come on. *Please*," I say in the loudest whisper I dare use. Halverson's ears are like satellite dishes on the sides of his head; we're sure he can hear us think.

Jen glares back at me in a way that I'm supposed to understand means there is *no way in hell* she's going to give Halverson the Big M.

"You've got to. I need to talk to you now." I practically split my lip, I'm mouthing the words so hard.

The thing is, I know in the end she'll do it. Jen isn't a coward. This is just the sort of thing she loves to pull off. She'll be bragging about it at break. I could never do it—I might go along with some of the stuff she pulls, sure, but I'm never the one who initiates things.

Last year, on our first day of seventh grade, they had us fill out these questionnaires in homeroom. There were a bunch of questions about our favorite subjects and interests and what kinds of clubs we might like to join. I was halfway through mine, neatly filling it out in pencil with careful an-swers, trying to make sure I got it all right and was giving an accurate picture of myself, when I looked over at Jen. In bright purple ink she had answered every question with a joke. For "What do you enjoy most about school?" she wrote, "Being absent." For which subject she liked best she answered, "Fire drills." For favorite pastimes and hobbies she said "BOYS!!" When Jen glanced over at mine she rolled her eyes, plucked my pencil out of my hand and filled in a couple of answers for me with things I would never say. I laughed with her until we got shushed by the teacher, but after the bell rang and Jen had run off to her first class, I stayed behind and erased her answers, then filled them in the way I knew I was supposed to.

Jen turns her head away from me and pretends to con-centrate on the blackboard, copying down the reading assign-ment and study questions. I wait. Sure enough, two minutes later Jen closes her notebook, smooths her miniskirt and walks up to the front blackboard. She waits politely behind

Halverson until he's finished scratching out the names of the Supreme Court justices in his crimpy, scraggly handwriting.

"Mr. Halverson, uh, could I, uh, talk to you in the hall for a second?" She's blushing! I can't believe it. Jen's sooo good at this; I could never blush on cue.

They step into the hall. Although I can see them from my desk, I can just barely hear them. I lean forward and cup my ears, trying to look as if I'm messing with my hair so no one will notice. All I need is to have the whole class leaning forward, trying to listen with me.

"Mr. Halverson," Jen says. "Casey's got a little problem. I mean, she's had an accident and she, you know . . . It's that time of the month and her skirt . . ."

Halverson starts to nod. He throws up his hands to keep Jen from saying another word.

Two seconds later they're back in class. Jen nods at me. My face sizzles as I get my stuff, tie my jean jacket around my waist and slip out the door. Jen is right behind me.

We slap our hands over our mouths and fly down the hall until we crash through the swinging doors and into the cold, wet-smelling girls' restroom.

"Can you believe we got away with that in Halverson's class?"

"Man, did you see his face? He turned beet red!" Jen says.

"*He* turned red; *you* could be an actress!" We slide down the wall until we're sitting on the dirty, pink-tiled floor, holding our stomachs, laughing.

I lean sideways and do a quick reconnaissance of the stalls. No feet; we're alone in here.

"I can't believe we pulled the Big M on Halverson. It was one thing doing it to Mr. Prescott last semester, but Halverson . . . He's so old."

Jen crumples up a piece of doodled-on notebook paper and tosses it onto the overflowing trash can. It tumbles out and lands in the drifts of wadded-up paper towels piled around the can. I wonder if the boys' bathroom is this messy? Probably not. Boys never wash their hands.

"Okay, so we're here, Casey," Jen says, after we've caught our breath. "What was sooo important that I had to humiliate myself with your supposed menstrual problems in front of the old guy?"

"I've been texting you all morning. Didn't you get any of my messages?"

"I forgot to charge it last night," Jen says. "So just tell me now."

Now that our little laugh is over I can feel my heart go back to being a big heavy sack in my chest. I know as soon as I tell Jen about this summer, it's going to be real. I didn't call her when I found out last night because I kept hoping Mom would change her mind. Besides, I knew Jen would have said, "Just tell her you're not going or that you'll only go for the usual two weeks. You just cannot be gone from here for the whole summer." As if I could do that, as if I could just say no to Mom, as if I had any say at all in what happens in my life.

I suck in a big gulp of air and say, "Mom's shipping us off

to Dad's for the summer." Instead of the indignant reaction and boatload of sympathy I'm hoping for, Jen gives me a mildly expectant look, as if I've just mentioned that I forgot my homework and I'm going to need to see hers. As if she even does homework.

I kind of jut my head in her direction to encourage a more appropriate response. "So?" she says. "You go every year."

My shoulders drop. "Yeah, but never for this long. Usually it's just two weeks. I'm talking about this *whole* summer."

"No," Jen says.

"Yeah," I say, and I can feel those hot tears coming fast.

Jen unclips her hair, grabs a handful of it and twists it around her fingers. She isn't about to hug me, or cry too, or anything like that. We're absolutely the best friends in the whole world, but we are not mushy.

"The *whole* summer?" Jen finally says.

"Well, eight weeks of it, anyway. It might as well be the whole summer. I can't believe it. I'm so mad. I had plans. . . . *We* had plans! How can Mom do this to me?"

"What about the photography workshop you signed up for?"

I give her a thumbs-down sign.

"What about our auditions for the band?"

"I know," I say.

"With *Matt.* And *Bobby!*"

"I *know.*"

"Can you just say no?"

"Not a chance."

We exhale simultaneously, long and loud.

"Is it just you, or PJ and Mike too?" Jen asks.

"All three of us are going. You know how Dad is always going off on these trips to study polluted lakes or dying sea snail populations? Well, this time it's sea turtles and he's staying on this island where they nest, so now we're spending our whole summer with him in—get this—Tartuga." Jen looks at me as if I've said Timbuktu, which I might as well have.

"It's not even in the *United States*. It's clear out of the country, right off the continent. It's in the Caribbean, practically in the next hemisphere. There's probably pirates there. And *bugs*," I say.

That morning I had looked again on PJ's globe at the string of Caribbean islands way south of Florida, which is *already* an entire country away from California, and I still couldn't believe it. Last night, just before dinner, when Mom was giving us the big news, she pulled out the globe and showed us the speck-sized islands in the Caribbean Sea. Mike was really into it, measuring the distance between the islands and California with his thumb and index finger like an inchworm. When I wasn't thrilled out of my gym shorts like she'd expected, Mom said, "The way you're acting, Casey, you'd think I'd sentenced you to three months of hard labor instead of a summer in paradise."

"I'd rather have hard labor," I said.

"What was that?"

"I said, 'Do you want me to set the table?' "

Mom had just looked at me like she *knew* that wasn't what I'd said at all, but she didn't have time for me then.

"So what happened to the usual Florida trip?" Jen asks.

She's using the end of her Bic pen to scrape the gummy gray junk out of the spaces between the floor tiles. The gunk is piling up accordion-style.

"Dad's taking a yearlong sabbatical from teaching at the college, so he and his bride, as Mom calls her, are using it to study the mating habits of endangered sea turtles or something like that. He could have gone anyplace he wanted, but *no*, he picks this island because these damn turtles are there, protected by the government. He's already been there a few weeks and now he expects us to spend our entire summer vacation there with him."

"Okay, okay, so you're going for the summer instead of the usual two weeks," Jen says, thinking. "We can handle this."

"Now you sound like my mom. She says it'll be a great experience. It's really just her way of getting rid of us so she can spend more time with her boyfriend, Roger."

Personally I think Mom's kind of in a rush to get permanently hooked up with Roger, maybe because Dad got married so soon after the divorce. I think she could do better than Roger. He's not even good-looking, like Dad. He's got a definite comb-over going on toward the back of his head and it's just a matter of time before it creeps up to the front and he's a full-out baldy. Plus he's boring. He gives way too much detail when he tells a story—and not the kind that makes a story funny or interesting. For example, if he's telling Mom something that happened at work, he starts off by telling her the exact time it was, as in "at three-oh-eight," what *tie* he was wearing, where he was standing in relationship to, say, the potted plants in his office, and exactly who else was there. Then he tells us every single person's name, *first and last*. Like anyone's going to remember, or *care*. By the time he's done reciting all these particulars, not to mention every coworker's genealogy, I start hoping for a 5.0 quake to hit—nothing catastrophic, just something to shake things up a little and prompt a change of subject.

"No, no," Jen says, snapping me back into the moment. "I meant, we can break your leg so you can't go, *or* we can run away and not come back until September." She's picking up momentum now. "Or we could fix it so that you *accidentally* miss the plane and your brothers go off without you. You're left here, your mom takes off on her trip with Roger because she thinks you got on the plane, and we've got your house and the summer to ourselves. No parents, no little brothers!" This last bit of genius really inspires her and she stands up and starts pacing.

"Yeah, that's it! I'll ask to go with you to the airport, you know, to see you off. Right when your plane is going to leave, we'll say we have to go to the bathroom, and *then . . .*"

"Oh no! The Big M again?" I say. Now we're both laughing.

"All right," Jen says, "that won't work. We could figure out a way to smuggle me on board with you. Then it won't be so bad. We'd have a great time! Maybe there's lots of cute guys there?" Jen's back down on the floor, giving me her big "cheer up" smile.

As soon as she mentions guys, though, I feel terrible all over again. Half the reason I don't want to go is Jen and all our plans for this summer. We had this great idea to start a garage band—the whole point of which was so we could hold auditions and invite the boys we like to try out. And we told Jen's older sister that we'd wash her car every week if she and her best friend would let us ride with them when they went to the beach—and they go all the time. Then there was my photography workshop—I even put down a deposit on that. I'm going to miss at least four parties I can think of . . . and just all the general hanging out I was looking forward to. I'll probably end up having to see all the good summer movies on DVD.

The other half of why I don't want to go is my boyfriend, Matt. We haven't made any public declarations about our boyfriend-girlfriend status, but it's, you know, *understood*. We've been hanging out together for almost two months, going to movies and games at school and stuff. We eat lunch together every day. He's been taking guitar lessons, so naturally we were going to "audition" him for our band. I've really been looking forward to being with him all summer.

Jen knows what I'm thinking. "Oh, Case, you know the old saying, 'Absence makes the heart grow fonder.' "

"Right. And you believe that? I think it's more like 'Absence makes the heart go wander.' I don't think I can go the whole summer without Matt." I can feel salty tears pushing against my eyeballs.

Jen kisses the back of her hand wildly and makes obnoxiously loud smacking noises.

"Oh, Matt!" she says in a fake French accent. "I love you so! Come weeth me to a tropical island and vee vill svim naked in zee moonlight and slow dance under zee pine trees."

"No, *pine* trees, you moron, palm trees, or coconut trees, or . . . oh, I don't know."

"I wouldn't worry about Matt too much, Casey. And since I know what you're *really* worried about," she says, tipping her head sideways and giving me a little conspiratorial smile, "I promise to keep an eye on Patty Harper while you're gone. I'll make sure she keeps those Maybelline eyes away from him." She bats her eyelashes for emphasis.

Just the *name* Patty makes my stomach flip over twice. Everyone knows she's in love with Matt. It's sickening. Plus, she's extremely cute. I mean *extremely:* cute clothes, thick wavy hair, a perfect shape, enormous green eyes, clear skin and, to top off the whole ensemble, a 34C bra size—and not a Wonderbra, either. I look down my chest at the completely unobstructed view of my lap. Yeah, I hate her.

Jen says, "Seriously, though, Casey, you know that if you guys can't manage to hold it together over the summer, courtesy of AOL and Verizon, then it isn't really true love."

As soon as she says that we both look at each other and roll our eyes.

"Oh, come on, Jen, that's a line our parents would use and you know it. Besides, there might not even be DSL on the island. Just think if I have to use . . ." I feign despair and let out a little screech, and Jen gives me a pretty good imitation of the doot-doot-doot Internet dial-up sound.

Before *that* possibility can sink into my brain, the bell rings, the doors bang open, girls pour in, cell phones vibrate, beep or play Beethoven's Fifth and our sanctuary is transformed back into the girls' bathroom.

2

Our school has two outdoor lunch areas and, even though there aren't any written rules about who sits where, everyone knows that only seventh graders use the area by the gym. The rest of us sit in front of the cafeteria. I like this arrangement because I can buy my lunch in the cafeteria, then slip outside with it. All the cool people sit outside.

The only problem is the seagulls. Even though we are a good forty-five-minute freeway drive away from the beach (and that's only if there is no traffic, which is never), there is this huge flock of seagulls that swarm around at lunchtime looking for scraps of food and, every now and then . . . SPLAT! All over the place. At least once a week someone gets it royal. It's disgusting, and it's a *lot*. Like a water balloon being dropped on your head, but full of something a lot worse than water.

I'm sitting at our usual spot outside poking my Turkey

Surprise (Surprise! No Turkey) with a fork, waiting for Jen and Matt. My fourth-period class, photography, is right next to the cafeteria so it's easy for me to get my lunch and get out here before everybody else even gets to their lockers. I can save the bench that way.

"Hey, Case, I'll be there in one minute, I just wanna get something out of my locker," Jen yells to me. Matt passes by her, giving her backpack a thwack.

He's so cute. This might sound corny, but every time I see him, my heart melts. I know you feel with your brain, that's what my science teacher says, but really, I can feel it inside my chest. Matt has long dark eyelashes and when he looks down they rest on his cheeks. I'd like to get a picture of him that way.

"Hi, Casey. I've got something for you," he says, holding a folded piece of paper up out of my reach so that I have to jump up and grab for it. I miss it and while I'm up, Matt sits down real fast in my spot and picks up my bowl of Turkey Surprise. He stares into it with a shocked look on his face.

"Oh *no*. Look at this! It's the Seagull Special. You don't want to eat this, Case," he says, real serious-like and concerned. "A bird must've nailed it when you weren't looking. You don't even want to *see* this. You can eat *my* sandwich while I get rid of this for you."

He hands me his brown sack and the folded paper, which I know is a note for me from my friend Gina. She sits next to him in his fourth-period geometry class. Matt's our mail carrier.

I always wonder if he reads them before I get them. I'm

really careful to only say things I'd want Matt to see but still make it sound like I don't know he's reading them. I tell Gina to watch it too.

"Give me my lunch back," I say to him, laughing. "I don't want your stinky old anchovy sandwich. I'll take the turkey, thank you." I sit next to him on the bench and he hands my turkey back. Jen arrives and sits on the other side of Matt.

"How many times do I have to tell you?" Matt says. "They're not anchovies; they're sardines. *Sar-deens*."

He unwraps his sandwich and flips open the bread. There they are, lined up like little corpses, six sardines resting on top of tomato slices on top of cream cheese. It's the weirdest sandwich I've ever seen.

And I used to think Jen was strange because she brought peanut-butter-and-pickle sandwiches when we were in elementary school. Matt shows the insides of his sandwich to Jen, who says, "Looks to me like you need a couple of pickle slices."

"You guys are nauseating," I say. I take my bowl of turkey and settle in. I'll read Gina's note in Ms. Castruita's English class after lunch.

"You know," Jen says, "I don't know how you can stand to kiss Matt after he eats those sandwiches. You might as well just go down to the Santa Monica pier and suck on one of the pilings."

She's rooting around in her lunch bag so, luckily, she misses seeing Matt's ear tips turn bright red, even though he and I both laugh at the same time and I say, "Fish oil is supposed to be good for your heart."

Matt is extremely busy chewing.

The truth is that Matt and I don't *kiss*. Well, we've kissed. In fact he's kissed me a total of seven times. But we don't kiss, at least not in the way Jen means, like making out for long minutes at a time. Practically everyone does that, I know. We just haven't, but not because *I* don't want to.

Matt's kind of shy when we're alone. In a group, no one would guess that about him. He jokes and kids around and seems just as relaxed around girls as he does around other boys. He teases Jen and talks to her as if they're old friends. But when it comes to him and me being alone together, he just clams up. At least when it comes to the kissing part. A couple of times I've wanted to just grab his ears and yank his face toward mine because I've gotten so frustrated waiting while he tips his head this way and that, looks around, says something completely unrelated to anything in the world, then *finally* kind of l e e e a n s *forward* . . . oh my god, it's enough to make me want to run and get Jen and have her give him make-out lessons. Well, not *really*.

Actually, I haven't even talked to Jen about this because I'd never hear the end of it. I'm sure she doesn't have *any* problems in this department. She's not at all shy. She would never sit around like me, patiently waiting for things to happen while she endured what amounts to *seven first kisses*.

"Fish oil is good for your heart, huh?" Jen says to Matt. "Well, maybe you'd like to bring an extra one of those little numbers to school tomorrow, Matt. You can give it to Bobby for me. Maybe it'll melt his heart. Whaddya say, Cupid?" Jen says, fluttering her eyelashes at Matt.

"Are you still mooning over Bobby? You should just ask

him to the Fourth of July picnic before Patty Harper does. I know she's planning to," Matt says.

He stuffs his empty sandwich bag and other lunch trash back into his brown paper bag and rolls the whole thing into a ball. Standing on the bench, Matt tosses the bag into the air above his head, makes a whistling sound as he brings his arm back like a bat and hits the bag like a baseball. The bag flies across the lunch area and lands directly in the trash can.

From across the yard three guys yell, "All right, Matt!" Matt sits down with a bow.

"Who told you that Patty's going to ask Bobby?" Jen says.

"Actually, she told me," Matt says. He takes a brownie off my lunch tray. "Bite?" He gets about half of it in his mouth and gives the rest back to me. I finish it. We may not be making out, but we're not afraid to mingle our germs.

"So do you think he'll go? Does he like her or what?" Jen is looking at me with this kind of anxious look as if I'm supposed to know what's going on.

But what I'm thinking is how come Patty told *Matt* that she was going to ask Bobby to the picnic? When did they get all chummy?

I'm also just realizing that the picnic is another thing happening this summer that I'm going to miss. Lucky for me Patty doesn't know that or she'd be asking Matt instead of Bobby.

Matt says, "Look, all I know is that Patty said she might ask Bobby. That's it. You just need to get to him before she does."

"Yeah, but what if he doesn't want to go with me cuz he thinks Patty might ask him?" Jen says.

Matt rolls his eyes. "If he wants to go with you, he will. If he doesn't, what difference does it make to you who he's waiting for?"

Clearly boys don't understand this kind of thing. They believe things are more straightforward than they ever really are.

Jen jumps up. "That does it," she says. "I'm going to find Bobby right now and tell him we're going together. I'll bet he's in the cafeteria. The four of us can share a basket. Right?" Then she takes one look at my face. "Oh, sorry, Case. I forgot. Well, I'm out of here. My absence will give you two a chance to discuss Casey's big news."

She stomps off looking more like she's on her way to tell Bobby off instead of invite him to a picnic.

"What news?" Matt says.

Great, leave it to Jen to spill my beans for me. I wanted to wait to tell Matt sometime when we were alone together— alone, alone, not alone together surrounded by three hundred kids chomping down lunch. I had imagined a romantic moment where he'd wrap his arms around me and tell me how much he would miss me. Something along those lines. Maybe a little making out. Something to think about while I'm gone. So much for that idea.

"It's about this summer," I say. Matt just lifts his eyebrows like, Yeah? So what about this summer?

The lump forming in my throat stings around the edges. My tongue feels like it's drawing back to my tonsils. Finally

I say, "Well, my mom, well, she's sending me off to an island this summer."

"An island? Wow. Cool. Where is it?"

Not quite the look of abject disappointment I was hoping for and had so carefully scripted in my mind, the look that would say *his* summer has just been ruined too.

"For practically the *whole* summer," I say, really emphasizing *whole*. "I won't be back till September."

For a second he looks like it's sinking in, then he gets a little smile in his eyes and starts singing, *"I'll send you all my love, every day in an e-e-mail, sealed with a kiss."* He's holding his hands in a prayer position against his chest and swaying back and forth.

I don't know whether to laugh or cry. I guess it shows on my face because he says, "Whoa. What's wrong with you, Case?"

"I guess I didn't expect you to be so happy about my leaving."

"Well, I'll miss you, but it's only the summer. I mean, you know how fast vacation goes. Plus, I'm working all summer at the playground. I'd hardly get to see you anyway. So see? It's not that I'm glad you're going; I'm actually jealous. *We'll* all be stuck here in the hot, smoggy city while you're in some tropical paradise." He gives me a big smile.

Great. First Mom, now Matt. Why does everyone keep using the word "paradise"? I don't see what's so great about leaving my friends and having to go off and cook myself in deadly ultraviolet rays on some tiny, remote island that I need a pair of binoculars to see on the world map.

No one gets it. It's not that I don't want to go to an *island*.

Who wouldn't? Balmy breezes, sandy beaches, blue water, romantic sunsets, the whole bit, sure. Sounds great. I love the beach and I'd be dying to go if my *friends* were going to be there with me making it fun, instead of my two little brothers and *my dad*. Not to mention a stepmom that I only met for the third time on the day she married my father.

Naturally, as I'm working up to explaining this to Matt without a catch in my voice, Patty Harper strolls up. Matt is now singing *"I'll see you-ou-ou in Sep-tem-ber. . . ."*

"Oh, don't worry, Matt," Patty says, turning toward us. She's wearing a really short skirt and, I swear, she kind of arches her back and tips her chin up so we get the full Victoria's Secret effect. "You won't have to wait till September to see me. We're going to be working together. I got a job as a proctor at the same playground as you."

My heart does a free fall into my stomach.

"Hey, that's great! Congrats," Matt says.

"Thanks," Patty says. "I'm really excited about it. I just love little kids, don't you?"

She tosses her empty lemonade carton into the trash can and scares up a bunch of seagulls. As they lift off and fly over my head, I can't help ducking like a spaz and throwing my hands up in the air. Patty manages to stand there calmly. Then she turns her head slowly to look at me out of the corner of her eye, as if I'm the lamest person on earth, as if it's just not quite worth the effort it would take to look directly at me. She looks directly at Matt, though, gives him a big smile, then walks away, making sure everyone in the lunch area gets a good, long look at those 34Cs.

3

This last week of school—my last in the civilized world—was supposed to be so fun; instead it's been a huge letdown. I've spent almost the whole week alone, a little foreshadowing of my summer, I'm afraid. My bummer summer.

We've had half days all week because of finals, but instead of hanging with Jen and Gina and going to the movies or whatever, Jen, as usual, didn't study for a single class. That means every day she's had to race home after school and study like a maniac for the next day's final.

Gina's caught up on school stuff, but she has a babysitting job in the afternoons so she's not free to do anything except talk on the phone.

And Matt, with whom I'd *really* hoped to spend some quality time before I left, is on the school paper, so he's been really busy too, getting out the last issue of the year.

I took my list of stuff I need for the trip and went to the mall by myself. That was okay, I guess. I was done a lot faster

than I would have been with Jen along taking a bunch of de-
tours into music stores and stopping at Mrs. Fields. I found
some perfect quick-drying nylon shorts and some T-shirts in
Caribbean colors. At least I'll look cute, even if there won't
be anyone there to appreciate it.

I really didn't need all this alone time right now, since
I'm about to do nothing but be alone. For eight long weeks.
Except for the company of my two charming and entertain-
ing little brothers. Oh joy.

When I called Gina this morning to bitch and moan
about my plight, she gave me one of her little pep talks
about looking on the bright side and making lemonade out
of lemons.

"Oh, Casey, if it were me, I'd be thinking of all the ways
I could use this time for self-improvement. I mean, think of
all the stuff you can do while you're there that you don't
ever get around to here at home."

"You're right, I could do a lot of staring at the wall and
crying into my pillow. I almost never have time for that
here," I say.

"For *example*," Gina says, completely ignoring my sug-
gestion, "you could use the time to get in shape. I'd be doing
lunges, crunches and push-ups so that when next semester
started, I'd look and feel great! I'd read at least six books—I
mean, you could have the whole summer list for school
read! Plus you'll have time to read anything else you want."

I imagine myself doing crunches under a palm tree while
duck-sized mosquitos take aim at my legs. Gina is still chirp-
ing into the receiver: "If you don't make up your mind *this
minute* to have a good time this summer, you're practically

guaranteeing that you won't. You need to focus on the good part, Casey."

I wonder which good part she means, the part about missing out on everything all summer, or the part about Patty Harper having eight weeks to flirt with Matt.

"I'm so jealous, Casey," Gina said. "I've always wanted to go to the Caribbean . . . have you been online yet and looked at any pictures? I checked for you . . . it's beautiful there. You should see the water—it's the most beautiful turquoise you've ever seen."

I know she's right about that. I've seen plenty of pictures on postcards and calendars of white beaches, pale blue water and sailboats gliding by in the distance. It's all very picturesque. What you also always see in those pictures is a perfect-looking couple walking hand in hand along the beach or standing up to their waists in the water, arms twined around each other, gazing at a big orange sun sinking into the horizon.

That's my point.

You don't see a lot of calendar shots of mortified teenage girls hurrying along the beach trying to get away from their little brothers, who are following them everywhere, kicking up sand and throwing soggy strands of seaweed at each other.

By the time we hang up, I decide Gina is right. It won't hurt to have a more optimistic attitude about this trip. I make a list of things I'll get to do there:

1. Push-ups
2. Practice using my new macro lens
3. Take at least one shot that's worth submitting to *Photography Magazine*.

Actually, I probably *will* come back with a lot of good photographs, I really *might* do some push-ups and I *will* get to see Dad, whom we haven't seen since Christmas—not counting the few hours we spent at his wedding. Dad spent our spring break on his honeymoon with Sheryl. Normally Mike, PJ and I would have spent that week with him. So I've missed him. He calls once or twice a week and we all get on the phone and talk to him. He sends e-mails, but it's not the same as seeing him in real time. Now that he's married, I have a feeling we won't be seeing him on every one of our school breaks anymore because he and Sheryl like to travel. It's nice for Dad that she's into the same kind of natural science stuff he's into and she doesn't mind spending their time off going places where they have to stay in tents and their sightseeing excursions consist of looking at tube worms or inspecting unusual fungi. Mom, not so much. She's more the nice hotel, mints on the pillows, keep-the-clean-towels-coming type.

No wonder they got divorced.

Actually, it wasn't just that they didn't like to do the same things. It always felt to me as if they were strangers—well, more than strangers, but not a lovey-dovey couple. Friends, maybe, but not even as good friends as Jen and I are. The only thing I can remember them ever talking about together, at least in front of us kids, was things that had to do with the maintenance of our house or chores and errands that had to be done. Anything else was about us kids and our schedules, grades or doctors' appointments. I don't remember my parents ever talking about things that either of them were thinking about—like ideas, or a movie they'd seen or a book one of them was reading.

But then, if I really think about it, I realize that my mom is all on the outside. She's always doing ten things at once and she's very good at almost everything she does. She was the top agent in her real estate office for practically six months in a row; she's the person everyone wants to have organize any kind of event; she belongs to a bunch of city organizations and volunteer groups. She knows about a million people. My dad is more on the inside. He forgets to get his hair cut so half the time he looks like he just rolled out of bed; he's always reading some science journal and then cornering one of us kids, usually Mike, and telling him about a new theory of this or that.

With Gina's advice running through my mind, and while I'm sitting here waiting for her and Jen to arrive so we can go get hot fudge sundaes, a Final Final Day tradition we have, I've been flipping through this travel book Dad sent about the islands. Lots of pretty pictures, palm trees and white sand, pretty pink sunsets and, oh, there's that happy romantic couple. Just one little problem, though. Lizards. Lots of them.

If you ask me, and of course no one did, there isn't room on this planet for me and even *one* lizard. Not that I'd annihilate all lizards just because I can't stand them. I've always thought there should be an island somewhere just for lizards. Jen always says, "Careful what you wish for." No kidding. Apparently there *is* an island just for lizards, in fact, over *one hundred* different kinds, and that's just where I'm headed.

"Hey, Island Girl!" It's Jen hollering through the screen door. "Yo ho ho and a bottle of hot fudge!"

I toss the *Reptile Review* onto my bed, grab my wallet and head out the front door.

Both Jen and Gina are wearing Hawaiian shirts in my honor and Gina has a gift bag with her that's decorated with starfish and tropical fish stickers.

Jen has a pink hibiscus flower tucked in her ear. She must have snagged it off the bush in our front yard.

"Very cute," I say. Jen hands me a flower and I stick it behind my ear but it just falls out. I don't have Jen's thick hair.

"So, are you packed and everything?" Gina wants to know.

"Well, so far I've made a list of what I need to bring and I've started washing all my clothes—"

"*Casey*," Jen interrupts with an exasperated sigh. "That was a rhetorical question. We *know* you've probably been ready for days."

I just laugh with them, but actually, it's not true. I'd just barely pulled all my summer clothes out before they got here. Notwithstanding Gina's advice, and my trying to follow it, I've been putting off packing because . . . well, because I just don't want to go.

On the two-block walk to the shopping center, where there's this fifties diner with a soda fountain, Jen says, "So, how did you guys do on the finals?"

"Except for geometry," Gina says, "I think I did well."

"I'm sure I flunked them all," Jen says.

Gina and I look at each other and roll our eyes because

we know she probably aced every one. "Right," we both say at the same time.

After we order, Gina hands me the bag and says, "Here, we got you a little going-away present."

I pull out a framed photo of the three of us sitting at this very same counter that the waitress took for us last year when we were here for Final Final Day. Also in the gift sack is a neon blue net beach bag with a zippered pocket on the outside and two side pouches for sunglasses and a water bottle.

"See?" Jen says. "You put your wet stuff in the net part and the water drains out. The rest of your stuff goes in the pockets."

"It's perfect," I say. "And I love the color. I'll take the photo with me. Thanks, you guys."

"We've got another surprise for you," Jen says. "After we eat, though." Our sundaes come and we dive in.

When they start talking about the school summer picnic and a couple of parties that are coming up my heart sinks. For a minute while the three of us were sitting here talking and laughing it felt to me like all the last days of school that I can remember going all the way back to the third grade. I always feel a happy, contented excitement because I know that warm days with long hours of daylight are stretched out before us and we can fill them almost any way we want.

Now I have the feeling that if this were a scene in a movie, it would be in vivid color and there would be some great music playing in the background and we'd be animatedly laughing and telling stories, but then the camera would pull away and the sound would get kind of distant and muted. I would slowly start fading to black and white and then to pale gray as Jen and Gina kept on talking, not noticing me as I dissolved right out of the picture.

"Hey, right on time!" Jen says, scraping the last bit of fudge off the sides of her sundae dish. She's looking toward the parking lot and I'm stunned to see Matt winding through the cars toward the diner. This must be the surprise. I'm so happy to see him, and very surprised.

"That's our cue," Jen says, making me feel as if I've said the whole movie fantasy out loud instead of just imagining it. She and Gina stand up and Jen grabs the check.

"Bye, Casey," Gina says, giving me a big hug. "Have a great, fantastic, best-ever summer but don't forget to miss us a lot and send a hundred postcards and remember to make the most of it. I'd give anything to be going with you."

"Watch out for sharks," Jen says. "Try to get a decent tan and grow out your bangs. You should never have cut them. Don't worry about anything here, I've got you covered. Patty hasn't got a chance." She sticks out her lower lip in a sad-face smile and when she hugs me hard she whispers in my ear, "I love you, Case. Be good." It makes my eyes fill with tears.

Matt, who was hanging back by the door, is now standing next to me, so I just thank them both, mumble something about e-mailing a lot and wave to them as they head out.

"Hey," Matt says.

"Hi."

"I didn't want to miss seeing you off. Jen said I could

barge in on the girl-thing, although she did make a big deal about how it was a privilege and not to get any ideas about ever doing it again."

"That's Jen," I say. "Do you want a sundae or anything?"

"No, I thought I'd just walk you home, if that's okay?"

"Of course." I gather up the tissue paper and stuff my beach bag and photo back in the bag and we walk out into the bright daylight. Matt asks to see what they got me and I show him.

He says, kind of shyly, "I got you something too." He pulls a little wrapped box out of his pocket. "I thought these looked like the sort of thing an island girl might wear."

Inside the box is a pair of silver dolphin earrings. I love them. I put them on right away and Matt shows me how they look in the side-view mirror of a parked car.

On the way to my house, Matt mostly talks about the school paper and how he's decided to work on it again come fall. After a little while we fall silent. I feel as if there is nothing important enough to say in our last few minutes. We walk the rest of the way without talking, just holding hands.

When we get to my house he says, "Well, I guess this is it. I hope you have a great time and that you take a lot of contest-winning photographs and that you'll miss me a little."

"I'll miss you a lot," I say.

Matt squeezes my shoulder and says, "I'm gonna miss you a lot too." Then he kisses me, but when I peek I see his eyes are open and he's watching the front door. He probably thinks my mom is home. Then he's just gone, turning the corner and disappearing before I can even tell him that the coast is clear and Mom's at work, that we could stand here kissing for a hundred years and that I wish we would. But I'm left standing there fading to gray, a lump in my throat, dolphins dangling from my ears and a long, lonely summer stretched out in front of me.

4

"Need some help?" Mom asks. She's been standing in the doorway to my room for the last few minutes watching me pack. I've been pretending I don't see her, which I know is mean, but I'm still so mad at her for ruining my summer.

"No, thanks," I say. I have my underwear and three bathing suits rolled up and packed around the edges of my rolling suitcase. Mom got it for me; it's kind of cool, like a wagon for off-duty clothes. This is the kind of thing my mom is great at. Right now, if I told her how much I liked this suitcase, she'd sit on my bed and spend the next fifteen minutes talking to me about how she picked this particular bag over some other one because of its features or how well the zippers work. But if I told her how thinking of the suitcase as a wagon made me want to cry because wagons make me think of little kids, and little kids make me think of Matt working at the playground all summer with Patty Harper,

Mom would just pat my hand and say, "Oh, honey, I'm sure all that will all work out just fine."

I've learned not to bring up stuff like that with her because it's too frustrating. That's okay, that's what girlfriends are for. Now, if I need some tips on how to pack, I've got the exact right mom for the job.

It was Mom's idea for me to put all my lotion, shampoo and sunscreen in Ziploc bags, in case any of these tubes or bottles pop open and make a big mess. Then she's got me putting all that bathroom stuff, plus one of everything (like shorts, bathing suit, underwear) in my carry-on backpack in case our checked luggage gets lost or delayed. I wouldn't have thought of that, and if my luggage did get lost, all I'd have to wear would be what I showed up in.

Of course, now I just have to decide what to bring. Half my closet is spread out on my bed.

I notice guiltily that three of the shirts on my bed actually belong to Gina. I meant to give them to her yesterday, but I came back to the house with Matt instead. I'll have to leave them for her to pick up, along with her birthday present, which is all wrapped and ready to go. My heart sinks when I think about the surprise party that's planned for her in two weeks. A bunch of us worked really hard on it—we got photos of her and messed around with them in Adobe Photoshop. We made her tall, we made her short, fat, skinny, we gave her green hair, we paired her up with Chad Michael Murray, we gave her weird glasses, we pasted her head on Jennifer Lopez's body. We printed the photos, blew them up and glued them onto foam board with funny captions. We did a bunch with just Gina's face, made her eyes real tiny and her nose and mouth huge and made masks out of them for all of us to wear when we yell "Surprise!" Gina has no idea. I would have loved to see her face. Yet another thing I'm going to be missing out on. *Damn.*

"You know," Mom says, startling me. Jeez, I didn't realize she was still standing in the doorway. "There's an old adage that says you should pack everything you want to take and then put half of it back in your closet."

"I'll figure it out," I say.

She looks at my bed and the clothes I have draped over the back of my desk chair. "You won't need even half this stuff, Casey. Why don't you break it down into categories?"

"Mom, I'll figure it out, okay?"

"Just trying to help," she says. "You could start with what you want to wear tonight on the plane."

"I'm wearing what I've got on."

"Those shorts?"

"Yeah."

"No, Casey. You're not wearing shorts on the plane. I think you should wear slacks."

In my mind I don't even *own* any "slacks," just jeans, khakis and cargo pants, but I say, "What's wrong with these shorts? Dad said it's gonna be really hot there and that we won't need much."

"When I was young, we wore dresses when we traveled." She's about to add something, maybe even tell me they wore white gloves and hats, but the phone rings and her face perks up like a dog's when he hears his dinner hit the bowl before she shoots off down the hall like a bullet.

Roger. You'd think my mom was sixteen the way she jumps when the phone rings and the way her voice gets all light and fluffy when she talks to him. I listen for a minute and realize she sounds too normal; it's not Roger after all, but someone from her real estate office.

In the two years since Mom and Dad's divorce, Mom's probably been on about twenty blind dates. Everyone she knows tries to fix her up. She's been seeing Roger for a couple of months already, which has been kind of a relief from the constant parade of nervous guys standing in our living room having to be introduced to Mike, PJ and me. Sometimes it's pretty funny. PJ, who's only seven, can ask some pretty embarrassing questions. Once he asked her date if he made a lot of money. Another time, when Mom's date showed up in a suit and Mom was only wearing "slacks" and a blouse, PJ asked, "Are you going to marry my mom?" That's the last time we saw *that* guy.

My other brother, Mike, Mr. Reserved, never says anything to her dates beyond "How do you do" before he excuses himself to his computer. On his way out of the room, though, he always looks out the window to see what kind of car the date is driving. After they leave, Mike will tell me about the car and why it's hot or not. Cars, gadgets and graduating into the Boy Scouts next year are what matter to Mike. He's ten.

I think Mom thinks she has to hurry and find someone because Dad got married already. Sheryl is younger than Mom, and I think that bugs her too. I'm sure not in a hurry for Mom to get married, especially to Roger, who would make family mealtime around here as interminable as first-period

American government. It's one thing for Dad to have gotten married—we don't live with him so it hasn't really affected our daily lives. If Mom gets married, well, I'm sure that will change a lot here at home—and not for the better.

Sometimes I want to ask her if she's even liked any of these men she's gone out with—and if she even really likes *Roger* for that matter—or if she's just so convinced that she has to be part of a couple to have fun that it doesn't really matter who the other half is. But talking to Mom about something like that would be like trying to explain to her how I feel about Matt. She'd rather talk about luggage and the best way to pack it.

I look at all the clothes on my bed again. Okay, Mom's probably right and I won't need half this stuff. I start by putting all the dark clothes back in the closet. I change out of my shorts and into jeans and a pale yellow T-shirt so I can pack the shorts that I wanted to wear tonight in my backpack. Maybe I can pull a sky-high quick change tonight.

By the time Mom comes back and starts her hovering in the doorway routine, I have almost everything put back in the closet and the rest stuffed into my bag. I'm pressing down on the top of the suitcase and inching the zipper closed when Mom says, "I want you to watch out for PJ while you're there, Casey."

"I always watch out for PJ," I say.

"I know you do, honey. But you know PJ, he'll want to run off and go swimming every minute, and, who knows, climb rocks and trees, and I just don't want him to get hurt. He can't play in the waves, or go swimming alone."

"I know, Mom. Don't worry. He'll be fine; we'll all be

fine. Unless you count being bored to death." I kind of say this last part under my breath, but of course Mom hears me. I can feel a "talk" coming on, but then the phone rings again and she's gone. That's Mom. She could never let the machine get it while she finishes what she's doing. She can't tell Dad that all summer stranded on an island is too long for her kids. She can't tell Roger she doesn't share his enthusiasm for golf, so she buys herself golf shoes and designer golf getups and drags herself around the course with him every week. She sprouts wings and flies down the hall when the phone rings.

I finish zipping up my bag and realize I forgot to pack the eight rolls of film I'm bringing, plus the blue beach bag Jen and Gina gave me as a going-away present. I'm still wearing the earrings that Matt gave me.

Jen, Matt and Gina are picturing me having a great time in paradise. All I can picture at the moment is me being trailed everywhere I go by my two brothers and a thousand lizards. Never mind that all my friends will be having a great time without me, probably with Patty Harper filling my spot, flapping her eyelashes at Matt every chance she gets.

Down the hall I can hear Mom giggling on the phone with Roger. It sounds like everyone's going to be having a good time except me.

The pilot just announced that we're flying over the Mississippi River. Whatever brilliant plans Jen might have come up with to keep me home this summer obviously failed. There's no turning back now. And there are no parachutes, either. I asked.

Outside it is just night. No clouds, no farms, no Mississippi River, just black. I bought two postcards at the L.A. airport that I plan to mail from Miami, where we change planes. I choose the Santa Monica Beach sunset card for Jen. It says "Wish you were here," and I cross out "you" with a marker and write in "I."

> Dear Jen,
>
> Well, I'm on my way. If u r reading this, the plane didn't crash and we made it at least to Miami so it looks like I'm really going. E soon, I'll be dying to hear about the 4th of July picnic. Who went, with who, and, you know, tell me everything. I miss you already. Mom says it won't, but I'm hoping my cell works on the island—I'll try texting or calling as soon as we've gotten to Dad's, which w/b B4 u even get this card! Bye.
>
> Love, Case

Now Matt. I'll send him the one with the Los Angeles skyline since he wants to be an architect one day.

> Dear Matt,

Hmmm. Delete, er, erase that—too formal.

> Hi, Matt!

No. That sounds stupid. Well, not sounds, but looks. Like I'm all cheery and have on a yellow smiley face. Which I don't.

Matt, Hi, I'm here at 30,000 feet . . .

Forget it. He'll just wonder why I'm writing when I haven't even left the country. Matt already thinks I don't appreciate what a great opportunity this is for me. Finally, at the bottom of Jen's card I write:

P.S. Say Hi to Matt for me. Thanks.

I'll write to Matt later when there's more to report. Besides, the postcard I chose for him is a mess now.

I should probably be trying to sleep since we land in Miami at 6:00 a.m., then change planes to reach Dad's by noon. Just in time for lunch, Dad said on the phone. He can't wait to see us. Actually, even though I've spent the last two weeks complaining about this trip, I can't wait to see him, either. And, being around Dad is always a nice change from being around Mom. Mom always seems a little tense and it's hard to know if she's about to get really upset about something or if she's just distracted and in a hurry. Dad is so much more relaxed.

After five excruciating hours of trying to get comfortable in a seat the size of my gym locker, there is daylight outside. I can still see last night behind us if I really smash my face into the window and look back. Ahead of us is dawn, Miami, the islands and, of course, all those lizards.

First I read three words of an article, then my head snaps forward because either Mike or PJ has kicked the back of my seat while they're horsing around. Then I whisper-yell at them to knock it off. I've had to whisper-yell at them to knock it off about a squajillion times. It's been like this for the last half hour. Finally, I unbuckle my seat belt, get up on my knees, lean over the back of my seat and whack PJ right on the head with my *Seventeen*.

Most everyone on the plane is still sleeping, or trying to, and my brothers are being obnoxious. It's so embarrassing.

PJ gives me such a hurt look when I hit him, though, that now I feel guilty. That's the problem with little brothers. They're total monsters whose sole mission in life is to drive you crazy, but they also have this almost endearing, and annoying, habit of worshipping you. Because of that, I can make them, especially PJ, feel really bad. I mostly try to use this power wisely.

In Miami we have to wait an hour for our connecting flight, and my brothers, who didn't sleep one wink on the plane, are now snoring loudly, draped over two seats each in the waiting area of Gate 9. People are looking at us.

I use the time to text Jen and Gina "This is it, I'm really leaving" messages on my cell. Luckily I remember the time difference so I send them to their e-mail addresses instead of their cell phones.

When our flight is called and I wake them, Mike and PJ stumble and lurch along until we've boarded the next plane for the last leg of the trip.

This new plane is small, only about twenty seats. And it has propellers! I'm such a chicken. I'd much rather be on the jet we just got off, the one where I could pretend that I wasn't even really flying since I couldn't actually feel the plane moving along at however many thousands of miles a second it was hurtling through the air. We're nowhere near as high as we were before. I don't even think they had to pressurize the cabin. This means if we start a nosedive, there won't be time to die of fright before we hit the ground (I always count on dying of fright before impact when I'm in a big plane). Instead, I'll see every minute of my measly fourteen-year life flash before my eyes seconds before we smash into the earth like a giant dart. That'll shut Mike and PJ up, I guess. Their seats are at the back. They're snoring away in stereo again.

We're flying out over the ocean and I'll admit, it's getting nice. The water is really blue, not like at home. In fact, in places it's so clear I can see the bottom. I can even see the shadows of clouds on the ocean floor—and the shadow of this plane. It's *definitely* too small.

When the pilot announces that we'll be landing in twenty minutes, I walk back and wake my brothers. The scenery has changed so much in just a couple of hours. We've flown over dozens of islands. White beaches fringe each island. The ocean is an incredible aqua-blue-green—a nice eye color if you could choose. The color makes me think of Patty and those green eyes of hers. She probably did choose the color; she probably wears those colored fake contact lenses. I wonder what else on her might be fake.

Mike whispers to me that PJ wants to sit next to me for the landing because he gets kind of scared.

Mike and I trade seats and I sit with PJ and make a big deal of pointing out the islands and how the clouds look like whipped-cream puffs.

"Just think, PJ," I say. "In no time at all you'll see Dad. And Sheryl, you liked Sheryl a lot, didn't you?"

"What do you think Mom's doing right now?" PJ says in a small voice.

"Sleeping. Her alarm is going to go off in about two minutes. It's three hours earlier at home, remember?"

"Oh yeah," PJ says. He doesn't look happy.

I know he's feeling that weird homesickness we all feel on these trips. Just before you get to Dad's you suddenly wish you were home with Mom where everything is familiar and where you don't feel so far away that you might actually get lost and never be able to find your way back to that tiny dot on the map that's Sierra Madre, California. The feeling goes away as soon as we see Dad at the gate all happy to see us and everything. But this year my homesickness isn't going to evaporate the minute we land, since what I'm missing isn't Mom, or our house, but my life.

PJ presses his face against the window as we begin our descent. There are several islands lined up in a kind of jagged row. He's trying to guess which one is Tartuga based on its shape, which he knows really well from staring for hours at the map that Dad sent him. I let him work on that and don't point out that only one island looks even remotely big enough to have an airport.

As we get closer I see that even the island with the airport isn't that big, nor is the airport. In fact, it looks like it just has one runway, and it's not even paved as far as I can see. As soon as we land I know it's not paved because we

bounce along as if we're in a Jeep and we've left the high-
way. Finally, the plane stops about three feet before blue
water, then slowly turns around and taxis back to the little
wood building that is the terminal. There is a covered area
to one side and two benches with people and luggage waiting. I see a sign that says GATE ONE, and a couple of chickens
pecking around. I make PJ move his head a bit and look
around as well as I can—I don't see any other gates, or run-
ways for that matter. I think of LAX, where we were just a
few hours ago, and how there are hundreds of gates and
whole terminals for each of the airlines, not to mention lay-
ered parking garages and cops directing traffic all over the
place. There are no cops here, just one guy pulling a cart behind him, probably to load up the luggage.

The first thing I notice when we get off the plane, besides that it's about three thousand degrees and unbelievably
humid, is that the woman in the Customs line at the Tartuga
airport is wearing lizards for earrings. At first I thought they
were rubber but, no, they're real. And they're *alive*. She has
one hanging by its mouth from each earlobe.

"Wow," Mike says. "Are those glued on?"

The woman smiles and squeezes the jaws of the lizard
clamped to her right earlobe. It lets go. In one of those ac-
cents that sound a little like there should be some music to
go with it, she says to Mike, "Now give me the finger." Mike
stares at her and I stare at him. At the same moment that it
dawns on both of us what she really means, she reaches for
Mike's hand and he presents her with his index finger. She
clips the lizard to it.

"Neato! You try it, Case," Mike says, thrusting the horrid thing at me.

Oh sure. Maybe in about a million years when that lizard's fossilized body is being dug up by some sorry archaeologist.

The woman pinches the lizard's head again and snaps it back onto her ear. I can't help thinking that being an earring can't be such a great job, even for a lizard.

She stamps our passports and asks if we have any food or live animals with us. I want to say: "Sure, I've got a boa constrictor in my bag. I usually wear it as a necklace, but then my face turns blue and clashes with my T-shirt," but I can see Dad and Sheryl waiting for us through the gate so I just say "No." Dad's waving like crazy.

PJ is the first to get to him; he takes a flying leap and lands right in Dad's arms. A genuine Kodak moment. Mike and I are right behind. Kisses and hugs all around.

Dad's really happy to see us, and, for this *one little minute*, I'm really glad to be here.

5

"First stop, lunch," Dad says as we cram ourselves into a taxi waiting at the curb outside the little airport. Not a yellow cab like you see in the city. This is a little white pickup truck with bench seats in back and a red-and-white-striped canopy.

"When we get to the island, you kids can have a swim before you unpack and get settled. You look hot." It's not a compliment.

No kidding we're hot. The humidity must be 150 percent. The sweat on the backs of my legs is starting to soak through my jeans. Who needs to go swimming? I can just wiggle around in my clothes and get the same effect.

As if he's reading my mind, Dad says, "I told you all you need here is a couple of bathing suits and some sandals."

I wish he'd told that to Mom. My hiking boots weren't a good choice either. I feel like kicking them off right now and pitching my sweaty socks straight out the window. The back of my neck is soaked and I have a sweat mustache. I'm starting to envy Mike and PJ's short haircuts. My hair feels like a Polartec blanket on my head and down my back. Sheryl, I notice, has cut her hair short since the last time I saw her. And she's wearing shorts and a sleeveless top. *She* probably would have insisted that I wear shorts on the plane.

"What did you mean when you said, 'When we get *to* the island?' " Mike asks. "Aren't we *on* an island?"

"Sure, but this isn't our island. Ours is . . ." Dad pauses dramatically while the taxi takes a bend in the road. Our whole view changes. "There!" Dad says, sweeping his hand out the window with a flourish.

Across the bluest, calmest water I've ever seen are three small islands, side by side. They look like the humps of a giant green sea monster. All that's missing is its head.

"Which one? Which one!" PJ wants to know.

"The middle one, Ginger Island. The big one is Monkey Cay and the farthest one, on the right, is Lizard Island. Our house faces Monkey Cay. You can't see it from here."

I can't see any houses. It looks like three deserted islands to me.

"How do we get there?" I ask. "On another plane?" I'm imagining taking another propeller plane over there and crash-landing on Lizard Island.

"You'll see," Dad says. Typical Dad. Sheryl winks at us.

Dad really is excited to have us here. He's uncharacteristically talking a mile a minute as we bounce along through the center of town in the taxi. He points out all the places of interest: the recycling center, the desalinization plant where they turn seawater into potable water, the dump where they burn trash, the library, the school, the clinic and the ferry dock in the main harbor.

What interests me the most is a tiny pink building with a white roof, about the size of the popcorn hut at school—the Tartuga post office. Not quite what I was expecting. I don't know what I was hoping for, actually, maybe a Starbucks with Wi-Fi. Nothing like that here—this place is definitely back in the twentieth century. I wouldn't be surprised if they still have dial phones.

The taxi lets us off at a little restaurant. Really it's just plastic patio chairs and wood tables under an awning that sticks out from what looks like someone's garage. It's called De Best Place, Dis Side.

"Conch fritters, to start," Dad tells the lady who appears from behind a screen decorated with tropical fish. She hands us each a handwritten, photocopied menu.

Dad says, "I recommend the flying-fish sandwich."

He must be kidding, but there it is, right on the menu under *House Specialties*. Both Mike and PJ order one.

"Casey?"

"Grilled cheese," I say. Then, because Dad looks so crushed, I say, "Okay, flying fish, why not?"

Dad grins like a maniac. Sheryl winks at me. She means *Isn't your dad cute?*, which isn't quite how I think of him, but I can see why she might. I can tell he thinks she's pretty cute too, the way he looks at her. They've only been married about three months.

Even though PJ took Mom and Dad's divorce the hardest at the time, he really liked Sheryl from the beginning—probably because she's pretty. That's probably why Mike likes her too. What I like about her is that even though she's been nice to us, and seemed enthusiastic about spending time with us the few times we've been with her and Dad, she doesn't overdo it. She isn't *too* nice, or *too* fascinated with what we're doing in school or what we want to eat or do. She doesn't gush over us or fake interest, and she actually listens to what we say. The men Mom dated before Roger all seemed like they were trying too hard to get along with us, to be curious about our lives when they just weren't. Why should they be? We weren't curious about theirs. Roger is only interested in Roger, so he's not a problem.

The other thing I like, so far, about Sheryl is that she's young and she makes Dad seem younger than he used to seem. They do a lot of stuff together and Dad sends us notes with photos of the two of them and they always look like they're having a great time—and the main thing is, they're having a good time together. As for Sheryl being my step-mom, it's impossible for me to think of her that way since we only spend a few weeks with Dad every year, one at Christmas, one during spring break and, usually, two weeks in the summer.

When I look at her and my dad, they just seem like newlyweds and the whole idea of kids doesn't really fit in with that picture. When she looks at my dad, I can see little hearts in her eyes.

I wonder how Matt looks at me? While I'm trying to remember how Matt looked at Patty Harper, that last day when she told him she'd be working with him, my brothers yell, "*Wow!*"

There's a huge splash in the ocean. "What was that?" I ask.

"Pelican," Sheryl says. She scans the sky a moment, then points to a huge bird that's just dropped down, as if for a landing. "Watch this one, Casey. There he goes!"

The pelican skims along the surface, just inches above the water, then soars way up, pauses in midair, kind of like a roller coaster just before the big drop. We hold our breath, waiting. After a long second, the pelican takes a nosedive and heads in a perfectly straight line toward the water. *Kapow!* He hits the water like an arrow and completely disappears under a big splash. When he pops up like a beach ball a minute later, his beak is filled with water. He tips his head back and tosses down his catch.

"*All right,*" Mike says. "Got one!"

The conch fritters arrive. When we ask Dad what a conch is, he just says, "You'll see, you'll see. They're everywhere." Whatever that means. This time I don't even look at Sheryl because I just *know* she's going to wink.

The fritters are big fat puffy batter-fried things that smell fantastic. I figure a gym sock coated in batter and deep-fried is going to taste good, so these should be delicious. I break one open with my fork. Inside it's all squished-up creamy stuff with little flecks of hot pepper and it's really tasty.

The flying-fish sandwiches are also good. While everybody's yapping—the boys are going on about their soccer exploits and how many games they won and how Mike's team almost made the play-offs—I walk across the road to the seawall hoping to cool off. Plus, I want to fire up my phone and see if I have any messages yet. Jen's probably sleeping in, since it's vacation, but Gina's up for sure by now. I flip open the phone, turn it on and wait for the musical greeting. Hmm. "No service." I walk five feet over in one direction—still nothing—then I move five feet in the other direction and pull up the antenna. Nothing. I have an awful, sinking feeling that Mom was right—she usually is about stuff like this—and my phone isn't going to work here. She said you need a special chip for it to work out of the country, but I really thought that since we'd be so close to the U.S. Virgin Islands, Verizon wouldn't be able to tell that we'd left the country. Maybe there's an invisible border out there in the ocean.

Or maybe the reception is just bad here. I'll try again when we get to Dad's. I put the phone back in my pocket; I don't want to be too obvious about checking it in front of everyone, since we did just get here, and that's the kind of thing that always annoys grown-ups.

I kneel on the low seawall and look into the water. Even here at the shoreline, where I'd expect it to be murky brown like at home, the water is as crystal clear as it looked from the plane. Unbelievable. I can see the sandy bottom perfectly. I can actually make out *individual grains of sand*. And there are long skinny fish with needlelike noses swimming around near the surface. The water is so still and clear that I can see their little black eyes swiveling around.

"PJ, come here. You'll want to see this," I shout to him across the road. He dashes over. I look both ways in a panic because he didn't. Then I remember where we are. The only car in sight is the taxi we came in, which is now parked off the road. The driver is nowhere in sight; it must be his lunchtime too. There's a goat sniffing around the tires.

PJ leans out over the low wall and peers into the water. "Wow, fish! And look," he squeals. "A crab!" Sure enough, a small green crab is making its sideways way up the wall. "Take a picture, Casey!" PJ says. I do, even though I know it won't turn out the way he's imagining, since I only have my wide-angle lens on the camera. "Let's show Dad," PJ says.

"Dad's probably seen dozens of them," I say. Out of habit I grab PJ's wrist before we head back across the road.

"Dad, Dad!" PJ yells. "We saw fish with pointy noses! Thousands of them!"

I tell Dad there were about five of those skinny fish. He tells us they're called needlenose fish. I'm sure he's kidding; they must have a real name, but PJ thinks that *needlenose fish* is hysterically funny and I'm treated to a panoramic view of his back molars, including the remains of his conch fritters. I don't ask what the fish are really called. I'm not that fascinated with fish anyway, unlike those pelicans, which are still out there divebombing, feasting on needlenoses, no doubt.

After lunch Dad says we can walk, so we collect our bags and trudge down the road. And I mean road. It's not like a superhighway or anything. It's about a one-and-a-half-lane dirt road and once every few minutes a little Jeep or taxi goes by, kicking up dust.

Every person who drives by waves at my dad and calls him by name, Paul, and he waves back. It's very weird. Dad and Sheryl have only been here about a month, but it's like they've lived here all their lives. I can just imagine walking down the main drag at home, where we actually *have* lived all our lives, and waving at people. I'm sure. Either someone would just stick a gun out the window and shoot you, or the police would come and escort you off to a place with pretty gardens and loads of crafts classes.

About ten minutes along, and after we've passed two goats and several chickens, we come to a small wooden dock jutting out from a rocky stretch of shoreline. Nothing else, no building or signs, no anything, just this little rickety dock with a rickety sailboat tied up to it. I go down on one knee and take a quick picture of it, making it look longer than it is with the angle of the camera. The boat itself looks to be about twenty-four feet long.

"Kids, meet Bob," Dad says. We stand there sweating, politely waiting for Bob to stick his head through the cabin door so we can be introduced. Standing around sucks. It's way too hot. At least when we were walking, we stirred up the air.

We're still standing there when Dad says, "Well, I know he's not much to look at but I didn't expect you to be struck dumb."

Finally, Mike says, "Oh, *Bob*, I get it! The *boat's* name is Bob." He walks to the end of the dock and looks at the back end of the boat. "Yup, it's Bob, all right." Mike looks at me and kind of rolls his eyes, but then he laughs. "I thought boats were supposed to have girls' names."

Dad's cracking up. He stows our bags in the cabin below and we climb aboard. He instructs Mike, who stays on the dock, how to untie the boat.

"Okay, Mike, when I tell you, just free the line from that

cleat and toss it into the boat. Grab hold of the shroud, step onto the boat and give us a good shove off the dock."

Dad turns the key for the motor and it coughs to life.

I can tell Mike wants to do this perfectly. He's concentrating so hard his knuckles are white as he grips the rope. He doesn't even hear when Dad yells, "Okay, Mike, let her go!" Mike just stands there.

We all yell, *"Mi-ike!"* and he jumps about nine feet, then unwinds the rope from around the metal cleat on the dock.

"Okay, son, toss the line into the boat and step aboard." Mike throws the rope but it lands in the water. Dad scoops it into the boat. Mike hops aboard but forgets to push us away from the dock. He looks pretty relieved to be in the boat.

Dad says, "All right, everyone, lean over and shove us away from the dock. Watch your fingers." We shove and slowly the boat moves away from the dock. Mike sits next to PJ and me on the bench in the cockpit.

When we've drifted off about ten feet, Dad puts the engine into gear and we putt-putt away from the dock and out into the blue-blue sea that separates Tartuga from the three islands across the channel.

I can't resist slipping my phone out one more time and taking a peek at the display. Still "no service." My optimism is dying fast. Mom was right. Jen will be so disappointed; she was sure it would work because when her dad goes out of the country on business, he sends messages home from his Blackberry. Looks like it's going to be e-mail only.

"Which is our island again?" PJ asks.

"The middle one. Ginger. You'll love it. It's the nicest one in this little island chain; it's got five beaches," Dad says. "Monkey Cay doesn't have any. Lizard's got three, but two are on the windward side."

"How's the cellular service on the island?" I ask.

"Cell service?" Dad says. "That's a good one, Casey. Cell service," he says again, laughing hard now. Sheryl winks. Damn.

Dad hands me the tiller and says, "Here, Case, hold this straight while we raise the sails. Don't fall off."

Believe me, I have no intention of falling off this boat. With these boots and jeans I'd be a quick lunch for some bottom-dwelling creature. Delivered.

Sheryl scoots over. "What Paul—your dad—means is hold the boat into the wind, don't fall off, or away, from the wind. You want to keep the wind directly on the bow. Look up at the masthead fly."

I look to the top of the mast and see a red arrow pointing straight ahead.

Sheryl says, "That's the wind indicator. Just keep that arrow pointing the way it is now, straight into the wind. If the arrow points off to the left or right, you've fallen off the wind and you'll need to head up or bring the boat back up into the wind by adjusting your course so that the arrow lines up with the bow of the boat."

Okay, I think. Don't fall off *anything*, not the boat, not the wind, not my seat, not the planet. Not a problem. I hold the tiller straight until I see the arrow pointing off and then move the tiller to bring the arrow in line with the wind. At least that's what I think.

Next thing I know the boat spins 180 degrees.

Sheryl takes the tiller and straightens the boat out. She says, "If you push the tiller to the right, or to starboard, the boat will go to port." To demonstrate, she points the tiller one way and sure enough, the boat goes the other way.

"It's not like a car," she says. No kidding.

Okay, I think, okay, I've got it. I take the tiller again and point it in the opposite direction I want to go. It works! Meanwhile, Dad's yanking on a rope and making the sail go up. "Okay, Mike, winch it up," he says.

Mike sticks a chrome handle into a round thing that looks like an empty spool of thread and starts cranking. The sail goes up the mast and now it's really hard to hold the boat straight. Dad yells, "Okay, fall off to port!"

Oh, sure, why not. And which way was that? And should I just go in headfirst?

I look at Sheryl hopefully and she says, "Turn the boat off the wind to the left, but remember to point the tiller to starboard." I do. The sail fills with wind and we're moving along much faster. Dad comes back to the cockpit and turns off the motor.

"We be sailing!" he says, smiling. "Blissful quiet." He's right. With the motor off it's really nice; all you can hear is the water lapping against the boat and every now and then the *kaplowww* of a pelican taking a lunch dunk.

When Mike climbs in beside me, I ask him, "How'd you know what to do?"

"Boy Scouts."

Sheryl says, "You guys want a quick lesson?"

"Sure!" we say. Then I notice PJ's pants are all wet.

"PJ! You're sitting on that wet rope. Move over here."

Sheryl picks up the rope that Mike tossed into the water when we left the dock. "The first thing you should know," she says as she coils the rope in her hand, "is that there are no ropes on a boat."

Uh-huh, right. As far as I can tell this boat is dripping with ropes.

"These are *lines*," she says. "This is a dock line, and the line your dad used to haul up the sail is called the main halyard. These lines," she says as she unwinds two other ropes—*lines*—that are wrapped around the winches on each side of the boat, "are called sheets."

Sure, I get it. If you want to go left you turn right. It's not a rope, it's a line, except that it's really a sheet, or maybe a halyard.

Dad takes one of the lines and begins pulling on it. In the front of the boat another sail unrolls and *fwap!* we have two sails up and the boat is really cooking now. In fact, it's starting to fall over!

"Dad!" I yell. "We're falling off!"

Dad laughs. "We're only heeling, Casey. Hold the tiller steady. It's okay. The boat can't tip over. I promise." Dad releases a few lines, yanks on a few others, the boat straightens up a bit, and we keep moving along.

Dad names everything on the boat for us. The first sail we raised is the mainsail. The other sail unrolls from the bow (pointy end) and is called the jib. Starboard is on the right, port is on the left and the back of the boat is the stern. The mainsail (or "mains'l," as Dad prounounces it) is attached on its leading edge to the mast, which is that tall pole in the middle of the boat. The bottom edge of the mainsail is attached to the boom. You have to watch out for the boom because when you change direction, it swings across the cockpit of the boat. It's probably named for the sound it makes when it smacks you in the head.

I can tell all three of us, even PJ, are trying really hard to get it all but I think Dad is forgetting that none of us has slept since the night before last.

After a while Dad says, "Okay, crew, let's tack. Ready about?" Of course we all just sit there like dopes. Even Mike, Mr. Soon-to-be Boy Scout.

Sheryl puts her hand over mine on the tiller and says, "Ready!" She pushes the tiller all the way to port while Dad releases the jib sheet and we make a ninety-degree turn to starboard. We're headed straight for Ginger Island.

6

Dear Jen,

Well, I'm here and I've got bummer news: NO
CELL. Even if I couldn't see the border, Verizon
knows I've crossed it, so we can forget about that plan.
And no phone either, just a VHF radio that we use to
call other islands or boats. The pay phone in town is $5
a minute! Oh, it gets worse: forget e-mail. Dad's got a
laptop but there's no Internet service on this island to
hook into. I know, I know, you're thinking I've washed
up in the Middle Ages and you're right! That's the
problem with "paradise."

The only people here are us and this old guy, Anderson, who's working with Dad on his turtle project.
That's it, just two houses, two docks and two big generators for electricity. And the turtles.

Oh, and get this, we get our water from a cistern.

It's like a well that collects rainwater—and dead bugs—under the house. It's pumped up through a pipe into the house, so at least we're not hauling water up in a bucket like pioneers or anything.

Dad's place is nice, though, and bigger than I expected. PJ and Mike each have their own rooms. Mike's thrilled not to have to share with PJ. My room is really cool. I've got floor-to-ceiling windows (all the rooms do) and I look out at the ocean on two sides. Everything is screens and wooden louvers. The floors are tiled, kind of like in your family room. Air-conditioning takes too much electricity so all the rooms have ceiling fans, which are essential since it's very hot here. And humid. Really humid. I mean, dripping-wet-every-minute humid. Dad says we'll get used to it, that we've only been here 2 days and we haven't acclimated. I hope he's right because every second I've been here so far feels like the gym locker room when our whole class has crammed in there after volleyball practice. It does smell better, here, though, but it's very sticky. I don't know why I wasn't expecting that.

Actually, nothing is the way I thought it would be. The island is a lot smaller than I expected—I mean, count the population! There aren't that many palm trees. Mostly there are these manchineel trees. They've got little poison apples—bright green ones—hanging all over them. If you even touch one you get a blister. Very dietetic.

The water is beautiful, but I knew that. It's just as

blue and calm as in all those photos of tropical islands we looked at. And it's warm. You can hardly tell the difference between the water temperature and the air temperature. We took our first swim yesterday right after we got here—we were all wilted from the trip and the shock of the humidity. Did I tell you already that it's about 100% humidity???

I'm writing fast cuz Dad's taking the boat over to the main island, where there's a post office. There isn't one here on Ginger so I can only mail things or get mail (hint! hint!) over there.

As soon as I finish this, Mike, PJ and I are heading out for a little island exploration and then a swim—which we'll need because of the humidity, which I may have mentioned. I'm pouring sweat just sitting here writing.

Please WRITE soon. You'll get the hang of it. You'll need a pen and paper, though. Ask your mom, she'll know what they are. :) And you'll get a cramp in your hand, like me, but you've gotta keep me up on what's happening at home. OK, gotta go!

I'm out of time and there's not even any room to sign my name, but who else does Jen know who's stranded thousands of miles from home without even the most basic modern conveniences?

I race down to the dock while I'm still stuffing the letter in the envelope and hand it to Dad. He's off to Tartuga for supplies. You really have to plan ahead around here. None of this running out to the market every other minute. Mom would hate it. She's always sending Mike or me to the corner market for something at the last minute, *while* she's making dinner. Not here. Forget having pizza delivered.

When I get back to the house, PJ and Mike are waiting for me. They're both slathered in sunscreen and totally outfitted for safari. Mike's wearing sunglasses, a floppy hat, the kind with a brim all the way around, a big stick he must've picked up on the beach—he probably hopes we'll be hacking away at bushes to make a trail—hiking boots, tan cargo shorts, a tan shirt and a bright orange whistle around his neck. PJ looks about the same, without the sunglasses. His whistle is bright green.

Actually, all three of us have whistles, though mine is chrome. Dad gave them to us this morning at breakfast. We're supposed to wear them all the time in case we get lost or need help. Otherwise he said we can roam all over the island on our own—it's not like there's traffic or kidnappers to worry about. Well, in theory we can roam on our own. PJ has to stick with me, so it's not like I'm completely footloose and fancy-free.

"Don't you guys want to wear your bathing suits?" I say. "You know we're going to want to swim somewhere along the way, it's pretty hot."

"We can swim in our shorts," Mike says. "They'll dry right away."

He's right about that, it's so damn hot. Plus, even asking him made me feel like I'm the mom instead of the . . . the what, the babysitter? That's what I feel like.

I have my suit on under my shorts, but I run in to get a hat and a T-shirt and smear a little more sunscreen on my nose. I already look like Rudolph just from being on the boat. I change out of my flip-flops and into some tennies while I'm at it. I think Mike might be a little optimistic about what kind of an adventure we're heading out on. On the other hand, I don't actually know what the terrain is going to be like. Maybe we really will have to forge our own trail.

"I think we should circumnavigate the whole island," Mike says. "Dad says we can take our time, stop for a swim and still go around the entire island in less than two hours. We can walk directly across in twenty minutes."

"Okay, Mike," I say. "Sounds like a plan. Which way do you want to go?"

"Counterclockwise," Mike says.

"What's that?" PJ asks.

Mike and I both draw big circles in the air to demonstrate and Mike says, "The opposite direction the hands on a clock go."

PJ looks at his digital sport watch and says, "Oh, I get it." Mike and I just look at each other. Well, okay then.

Dad told us the next beach is only about ten minutes from the dock. Yesterday we swam at the main beach where the dock is, Turtle Beach. In the afternoon, Dad took us to another beach, White Bay, where the turtles live and where Anderson's little house is, in a ways from the shoreline. That was clockwise from here, which I'm sure is why Mike wants to go in the opposite direction. Otherwise we wouldn't be like real explorers going off into the great unknown.

I'm sure the other three beaches have names, but Dad

said he didn't know them. He's like that, kind of absent-minded about everyday things like street names, his phone number and where he put his keys—even his car. He doesn't have to worry about that around here. No keys, no phone, no car. It was Sheryl's idea that part of today's expedition should include naming the rest of the beaches and anything else we see fit to christen, even though I suspect she actually knows the real names. She's just trying to make it fun for Mike and PJ. She probably couldn't think of anything that would make all this fun for me. I can. A big tidal wave that would wash PJ and Mike out to sea. Okay, that's mean, I think. Silently I take it back . . . but I can't helping shooting a look out to the sea from the corner of my eye. Flat as a tennis court.

We haven't gone ten feet down the sandy trail away from Dad's house before PJ yelps and starts hopping up and down. "Hey, ouch!" he cries.

Mike is already down on one knee inspecting PJ's ankle. I join him. It's a sprig of jumping cactus. Dad warned us about these plants . . . these, the stinging nettles, little wasps called jack spaniards and the stinging, but not poisonous, scorpions. Maybe we ought to rename this Hazard Island, I think.

Dad didn't mention lizards, but I've seen plenty of those, too, shooting across the walkways and sunning themselves on the ledges around the patios. They give me goose bumps, even in this heat.

Mike's trying to delicately dislodge the cactus thorns from PJ's ankle and boot. What happens is that as you walk by one of these low-growing, trailing cactus plants, one little sticky needle will get caught in your skin or your clothes and the whole spindly branch breaks off the main plant. It seems as if it purposely jumped right at you. Hence the name. Trying to get them out is tough because they stick to anything they touch, especially your fingers.

Mike pulls some tweezers and a small square of leather out of his pocket. He pinches the leather square to hold the cactus and uses the tweezers to pull the stickers out of PJ. Of course the cactus sticks to the leather. Then Mike has to pry that off with the tweezers. I'm pretty surprised, and a little impressed, that he's come prepared with tweezers and leather—who would have thought of that? Not me. I wonder what else he has in his cargo pockets.

After a few minutes he has the whole thing free, dangling from the tweezers, and he flings it as far as he can into the trees.

"You've got to keep your eyes on the trail, and stay in the middle," he tells PJ. PJ gives him a very serious nod as if to say, "That's a good tip, I'll do that. Thanks."

We soldier on.

We head along a sandy trail through a cactus patch—very carefully, though these are regular upright cactus and they keep to themselves. Then the trail we've been traveling on opens up to a little beach that isn't much longer than our backyard at home.

"This should be called Cactus Beach," PJ says.

"It's not a very big beach," Mike says. "How about Cactus Cove?"

We agree and do an official dedication by jamming a

stick in the sand and declaring the beach Cactus Cove in deep, booming and really fake voices. Well, they do. I watch.

We're all hot so we peel out of our extra clothes and wade into the water. Even though we were in the ocean yesterday, it surprises me again how warm it is. At home, the ocean is freezing by comparison. Not to mention rough. Here it's as flat and smooth as a swimming pool, and almost the same color. The salt makes the water feel silky, and makes us very buoyant, as if it would be impossible to sink. I'm sure it is possible, though, so I keep my eye on PJ, who likes to float with his face in the water until he runs out of air. But there are no waves or current to take him away so I don't have to worry too much.

After we've splashed around a bit and cooled off, we decide it will make us too hot to put our shirts back on, so we leave them in a neat pile under a tree, figuring we'll come back for them later—something we could never do at home, of course. They'd be gone in a flash. We just put our shoes on and continue to the other end of the beach in our already-dry shorts.

At the end of the newly christened Cactus Cove we come up against a small hillside that creates a point. There's a large flat rock we have to climb over and a nicely cleared path beyond it. Poor Mike has no need for his stick. The boys name the rock Flat Rock—they're not too inventive, I'm discovering—and we trudge up the hill and back down the other side onto the next beach. Mike and PJ immediately decide this should be called After Beach, because it comes *after* Cactus. As I said, not too inventive. They launch into their claiming routine, same booming voices, new stick.

They look disappointed that again I'm not participating in the ceremony so this time I clap enthusiastically.

This beach is about twice as long as the last beach (now *there's* a name!), which is still not very long. That's how it is here, much smaller in scale. I can practically lie with my feet in the water and my head in the shade of the trees that rim all the beaches. The sand here is different too. It's white and powdery and a fine film of it clings to my feet and up my ankles, making me look as if I've been dipped in sugar, like a cookie. At home the sand is coarse and looks like dirt.

"Isn't this fun, Casey?" PJ says.

"Sure, PJ."

"But really," he says. "Don't you like this place? It's a lot better than at home, isn't it?"

"Well, it's a lot different, that's for sure," I say. I might be willing to admit that it was better here if there were something to do besides name beaches and drip sweat.

"I like it here," he says.

"Good, PJ, I'm glad you like it. You should write to Mom tonight and tell her all about it."

"I will. Do you think she'll like the names we picked?"

I'd also think it was better if there were someone here with whom I could have a normal, sensible conversation. And who wasn't related to me. And who wasn't only seven years old.

"I'm sure she'll think the names are inspired, PJ."

"Well, it sure is pretty," he says.

It's very beautiful here, I'll admit. I'll write to Gina and tell her that. I'll give her the full description of all the different and brilliant shades of blue—the sky, the water at different depths and the bright green manchineel trees. She'll like that, too. She'll think I've come around and taken her "Make the Most of It" attitude. But I haven't, really. I mean, sure, I can see how gorgeous it is—anyone could— but I'm watching Mike and PJ jam sticks in the sand and dash in and out of the water, giggling and pointing things out to each other and I'm thinking that this is *it*. This is what my whole summer is going to be. Me circling the is- land, naming rocks and keeping an eye out for lizards and my seven-year-old brother while Mike practices his Boy Scout skills on wasp stings and attack cacti.

By the time we've made our way along the rocky edge of the shoreline and can just see the next beach on our itiner- ary, we're so hot and thirsty that we decide to cut across the island to the house for cold drinks. We didn't think to bring water with us. Some explorers we are.

And, I hate to disappoint these guys, but I'm planning to take a little nap this afternoon. We can save the rest of the exploration for tomorrow. I mean, if we do the whole thing today, what will there be to do for the next seven weeks, five days, fourteen hours and nineteen minutes?

There are ready-made trails everywhere on the island, crisscrossing and leading off in every direction, so Mike's a little disappointed, but he keeps his stick at the ready, alert to jumping cactus and anything else that might leap into our path.

What crosses our path is Anderson, Dad's helper. We met him briefly yesterday when we arrived and Dad intro- duced us. He's tall and skinny and probably not much older than Dad, but he seems older because of the way his chest has that caved-in look and his back is rounded over like a vulture's. There's something about him I don't like but I haven't figured it out yet. Maybe it's just because he mumbles when he talks so it's hard to understand what he's saying, and you wonder if he's saying something mean. To me, everything he says sounds like "Errrr grmpfph."

"Hey, Mr. Anderson," PJ says, even though Anderson is his first name. "We discovered two beaches already and we've named them. Do you want to hear the names we picked?"

"Errr grmpfph," Anderson says, looking at his shoes, which are crusty-looking canvas tennies with salt rings along the sides and no laces. He's wearing a floppy hat like Mike's, long pants and a long-sleeved shirt. I'm sure that saves on sunscreen, but he's gotta be roasting under all that. I notice he doesn't wear socks, though.

Mike and PJ start in with their names and the reasoning behind them but after a minute it becomes obvious that Anderson just doesn't care and their voices dwindle down and then fade out, like at the end of a track on a CD. I feel a little sorry for them. Finally we're all just standing there staring at each other. Well, *we're* staring. Anderson is shifting his weight and looking in every direction but at us. Mostly at his shoes. Maybe that's what I don't like, he doesn't seem to be able to look any of us in the eye.

"Are you going to feed the turtles this afternoon?" PJ tries.

"Already fed," Anderson says.

Okay, that's our cue, I think. "Well, we'll see you later," I say to Anderson, and signal my brothers that we should move along. Anderson doesn't say anything, but he sort of waves his hand—at least I think he waved. Maybe he saw a mosquito.

When we get back to the house, and after we've gulped down about a gallon of ice water each, Dad and PJ head off to see the turtles. PJ took an instant liking to the turtles when Dad first showed us around, and he wouldn't dream of missing a chance to lie on his stomach on the dock staring into the water at them. Can't quite see the thrill of turtle gazing, myself. They don't do much. They hang around the bottom until they need some air, surface, take in a gulp or two and go back down. It's not overly stimulating entertainment.

They're penned in by weighted underwater nets at the shoreline in a large section of White Bay where it's deep and, except for the grass, which is called turtle grass, the bottom is sandy. I may not find them fascinating, like PJ, but I sure sympathize with them. Their friends are out there in the ocean somewhere, doing whatever turtles do, and these guys are stuck here. I know it's for their protection, though.

Mike has a book on nautical knots and he's lying in the hammock in the shade practicing with a length of dock line. I can hear him talking to himself, "Over the top, around the bend, through the loop and pull." Then, "Rats. *Over* the top, around the bend . . ."

Fine with me. I've been spared having to traipse around the rest of the island this afternoon, staking claims on the various beaches. It's way too hot to be outside. I'm happy to lie here on my bed with the louvers half-closed listening to the ceiling fan go *shoom, shoom, shoop, shoom, shoom, shoop,* as it does its thing.

I wonder what everyone at home is doing, three hours earlier. Jen might still be asleep. She can sleep till noon, no problem. Or maybe she and Gina talked Jen's sister into a ride to the beach and they are on their way right now.

Well, I was on two beaches today, I tell myself. And really pretty ones.

So what. I'd rather be home with them, laughing and singing at the top of our lungs with the radio, heading down to Seal Beach where there are candy wrappers in the sand and the water takes your breath away, it's so cold.

If I could use my phone I'd call them and tell them about the jumping cactus and the crystal-clear water here, and how it's so warm it feels like a heated pool. All this island stuff would be nice if I had someone to share it with. Someone my own age.

I think about doing a few push-ups and then writing to Gina with a report, but instead I start thinking about Matt. He must have started his job at the playground yesterday. As soon as he comes into my mind, though, so does Patty Harper, all cute and tan in little board shorts and a tank top . . . I can see it—*them*—perfectly. I close my eyes. Forget push-ups. Now seems like a good time for that nap.

7

Hi, Matt—

The painting on this notecard is the island of Tartuga. We're actually staying on a small island called Ginger directly across the channel. Except for the houses and other buildings, Ginger looks exactly the same. The water is an indescribable turquoise blue (thank goodness for cameras), very calm and really warm! The sand is white powder and the sky is not flat and colorless like we're used to, but a changing landscape of fat white clouds in constant motion against a blue background. Great for photos.

We are the only ones on this island. Well, us, this man who works for my dad, hundreds of birds, Dad's turtles and 17 million mosquitos. We've been sailing a couple of times. You'd like that. Otherwise, there's not much to do here. Glad I brought a few books! Jen *probably told you we don't have phone or Internet service so I really feel far away and cut off. I miss all you guys.*

How is your job at the playground? Do you like the little kids? I feel a little like a proctor myself since I've got my own little kids to watch. Of course there's only two of them. I'm sure your job is harder. Hopefully you're still getting to practice guitar and have fun. I'll be happy to get to see a movie when I get home. There's nothing like that here.

Sorry I don't have much else to say; there really isn't much going on here, it's awfully boring. But pretty. :)

Casey

On a postcard of a white beach that could be any beach on Ginger, I write:

Dear Mom,

Yes! It really does look like this. And yes, we're all fine, everyone's behaving and we're all wearing sunscreen like barbecue sauce. Mike and PJ are having a great time. Mike likes getting to explore the island, PJ can't get enough of Dad's turtles and both boys love having their own rooms. They're not going to like having to share again when they get home. Time to move!

Everything here is very beautiful but you'd go crazy in about eight hours because there wouldn't be much for you to do. I hope you're having a nice summer.

Love, Casey

I spend about two minutes trying to decide if I should put "Say hi to Roger," but decide not to. I figure not mentioning Sheryl is enough.

"Can we go see the turtles now, Casey? You promised."

"Okay, PJ. Just let me write one more postcard. Get your shoes and tell Sheryl we're going. I'll meet you at the Big Rock."

Besides naming beaches this past week, Mike and PJ have named every tree, bush and rock on the island. Since there are no roads or buildings, we've been using things like trees, rocks and forks in the footpaths to say where we'll be. It's working out pretty well. Even Dad and Sheryl have started using the names the boys came up with during our exploratory excursions.

I know that PJ takes forever to get his shoes on and the sunscreen rubbed into his nose and ears so I decide I have time to write a real letter. I have another postcard I picked up in Tartuga—an aerial shot of the island chain. I'll stick that in with my letter since I don't have any developed photographs to send yet.

Hey, Gina!

I've circled our island, Ginger, on the enclosed postcard. It's not a very big island, but it's just as beautiful as you thought it would be and much more beautiful than I expected. There, I said it. Are you happy? JK! I've already used up all the film I brought. I'm afraid if I don't come back with a bunch of photos, no one will believe me when I try to describe it. I need a thesaurus just to figure out all the ways to say blue. The sea is like a giant, salted swimming pool, turquoise and calm. Some afternoons we come out to the bay and it looks like someone laid a huge piece of Saran Wrap across the surface of the water.

I've swum every day—it's really hard to stay out of the water because it's so warm! And it's so clear I can see my toes perfectly, even if I'm standing up to my nose in the water. We've also hiked all over the island three times, so maybe I really will come back in great shape. Okay, okay, so you were right about a couple of things. It's very beautiful, yes, but I was right about some other stuff. Like how lonely I'd be for you guys. And, believe me, I am.

I haven't heard from you or Jen yet (or Matt!), but I'm hoping to soon (oh, please!) . . . I'm really desperate for news as it is pretty bleak around here company-wise. I mean, I've got Mike & PJ with me all day. You know how that is since you've got brothers yourself. Zzzzz. Dad's great, and Sheryl is actually easy to get along with. She likes games, so in the evenings we've been playing Scrabble or Pictionary, which I like too. That makes nighttime tolerable. Note I did not say Loads of Fun. Just tolerable. Once night falls there's nothing else to do. Because of that, I've been getting up a lot earlier than I'm used to, to make use of the daylight. Jen would hate that. ;) The rest, the beaches and the swimming, you'd both like.

I just wish you and Jen were here with me. We'd have such a great time. I keep wondering what you guys

are up to, so please, please write to me. I'm stranded
out here with no electronic means of communication . . .
as I'm sure you've figured out by now. Otherwise I'd
be calling in between doing my push-ups! :)

xxoxo Case

After I sign my name, and just so I won't be such a big fat liar, I drop down to the tiled floor and do one push-up, which, as it turns out, is all I can do.

PJ ends up having to wait for me, but only a minute. We walk down the sandy trail that winds through the island a bit, then spills out onto After Beach. We follow the shoreline until we get to the point, then turn left into a thicket of sea grape trees and cut over a small hill to the west side of the island, where White Bay is, and where the turtles live.

This whole walk takes about twelve minutes. There's a faster way directly from Dad's, along a stony path right in front of Anderson's house, but we like the scenic route. Besides, by taking the long way, we avoid running into Anderson and going through the whole mumbling, eye-avoiding, shoe-inspecting routine. I've decided he really is creepy and it's easier to be polite to him when we don't have to talk to him. If he's at the turtle pen when PJ and I arrive he usually skulks off. If I see him first I usually turn around and go somewhere else.

Dad says he's hoping Anderson's sister will visit with her kids later in the summer. If she's not like Anderson, that might be nice, especially if there's a seven-year-old in the bunch who PJ could play with instead of hanging around with me. PJ's sweet, but he's not my first choice of someone to hang with. Not that there's a long list of better choices around.

White Bay is the longest beach on the island. At the far end, alongside a floating dock, is the turtle pen. There are eleven turtles in there right now. I know because PJ counts them every single time we come here, which has been every day for the past week and a half. Most of these turtles are healing from injuries; when they can manage on their own again they'll be let out. Dad and Anderson tag them all before they're released; that's how they keep track of their traveling patterns and stuff.

PJ runs ahead, plops himself down on the dock alongside the pen and starts counting.

"You really like these guys, don't you?" I say, sitting down next to him.

He tosses a piece of cracker into the air for one of the two seagulls that hang around the dock. Mike's named them Ozzie and Harriet because they're black and white, like that old show on Nickelodeon. I try to remember to wear a hat whenever they're around.

When I think about where these seagulls get to hang out, I feel a little sorry for our city seagulls at home who spend their days scavenging in our school lunch area. I wonder if they know how their Caribbean cousins live.

"The turtles remind me of Coco," PJ says.

Sure. I see the resemblance. Coco, PJ's Siberian hamster, is about three inches long and looks like a mouse someone flattened with a frying pan. He has long whiskers, beady black eyes, buckteeth and a teeny white tail. The turtles are about three feet long and almost as wide. They have heads the size of grapefruits and huge eyes with heavy lids. Their shells are an interesting green-brown color with a pattern of squares over their backs. The skin around their necks is loose and wrinkly, kind of like my grandmother's.

"You miss Coco, don't you?"

PJ nods solemnly and tosses another piece of cracker at the second gull, which has stepped up for his turn at the treats. Whether it's just these two gulls or there are twenty, they line up politely on the dock or overhanging rock and step forward, one at a time. When the first in line catches the bit of bread or cracker, he flies off and the next one takes his place. The rest wait their turns without complaining.

Maybe it's the turtles' tails, I think. It's a stretch, but their tails are short for such big creatures, and, well, maybe to PJ they are similar to hamsters' tails—in their shape, I mean—triangular.

"Probably the turtles' tails remind you of Coco, huh?" I try.

PJ looks at me like I am a total idiot. "Nooo," he says. "Turtles don't look anything like hamsters." He says this kind of slowly as if I really am the stupidest person on the planet and he wants to make sure I completely understand. "It's cuz they're *alive*. Like the seagulls. *They* remind me of Coco too."

Okay. So sometimes a seven-year-old's philosophy is a little over my head, but I can see why PJ likes to visit the turtles. We never see stuff like this at home. And as reptiles go, the turtles are sort of appealing. They look like they can't possibly swim. In fact, they kind of bob along, doh-dee-doh-dee-doh, but when they want to, they can turn on warp speed and split.

Dad and Sheryl talk about the turtles all the time so I've started feeling pretty friendly toward them. Not like PJ, though.

Besides taking care of the turtles every day, Dad spends a lot of time entering information about them on his computer. He goes to Tartuga every couple of days and enters his tracking data into a computer at the small marine biology office in town. He also downloads information that has been gathered by other people in the project who are tracking similar turtles on other islands. Then he comes back here and messes around with the figures. The whole idea is to try to monitor the turtle population and figure out how to keep it from getting too low.

Sea turtles have some natural predators, like sharks, but being snacked on by sharks isn't what is threatening their population. It's us. Fishermen put out huge nets to catch schools of fish, not turtles, but the turtles get snagged in there and even though some fishermen try to release them, a lot of times the turtles are injured or they drown. That's how Dad gets some of his turtles. Then there's the trash. Turtles eat jellyfish and, to a turtle, a plastic bag floating around in the ocean looks a lot like a tasty jellyfish. If they swallow a plastic sandwich bag they can choke and suffocate. There are also large sections of torn-up fishing nets floating around in the ocean and the turtles get tangled up in those. On top of all that, there are the poachers. The turtles are protected so it's illegal to catch them, but of course it's illegal to rob a bank, too, and people still do that. The poachers catch and kill the turtles for their shells, which they sell to people who make combs and souvenirs out of them. Dad says they don't even eat them, although they are edible—they just cut their shells off and throw the bodies back into the sea. Now I understand what it really means to say something is sickening. It's literally *sickening* to think about what happens to these creatures.

I never really knew anything about poaching until Dad started telling me about the turtles. Dad says the same kind of thing happens to elephants in Africa. Poachers will kill an elephant just for its tusks. They cut off the tusks, then leave the animal to bleed to death. I almost can't think about this stuff, it sounds so awful. I certainly don't want PJ thinking about it, since he's so attached to the turtles here. Dad's turtles are safe, though.

Anderson helps Dad with the turtles some, but he has a lot of maintenance work to do around the island so Dad's been thinking he might need some extra help. I volunteered, but Dad says he needs some real muscle, and besides, my job is keeping PJ out of trouble. Luckily, between swimming and meals, PJ is happy to hang out at the turtle pen at least twice a day. I usually bring a book and sit in the shade while he chats with the turtles.

Twice while we've been swimming, we've seen a sea turtle surface out in front of us. They have to come up for air about every forty minutes. We hear the water break quietly when they stick their heads up. If we're close enough, we can hear them take a breath. It sounds like a big sigh. PJ cracks up every time. By next week, I'll be like PJ, counting turtles and mooning over seagulls, I'll be so bored out of my mind.

Every day has been the same. We get up, eat breakfast, tidy our rooms, then head outside. Sheryl is working on an article about the turtles for a science journal. She also does reports for Dad using the data he collects. We try to clear out early so the house will be quiet for her. We hike a little, check things out, name a few rocks, go swimming, visit the turtles. Then we come back and Sheryl makes lunch. We swim some more, or I read in the shade while Mike and PJ swim, visit the turtles again, then dinner, we clean up, douse ourselves with mosquito repellant, play Monopoly or Pictionary, read a while, then go to bed. I mean, *really*.

"Do you think this turtle's exstink?" PJ asks, watching the biggest turtle swim back down to the bottom of the pen to munch some turtle grass.

"Extinct, PJ. Ex-*tinct*. And no, he's not. He's right here in front of us. He can't be extinct. And one turtle doesn't become extinct. A whole bunch of them do."

"Like those?" He points to a little group of turtles that are hanging out on the other side of our floating dock.

"Kind of, PJ. What I meant was, a species of turtle becomes extinct. If all the turtles in the world like these turtles died, *then* they'd be extinct. Get it?"

"These turtles won't die, will they?" he says.

"No," I say.

"Do you think I could stand on one?" He looks at me really hopefully. He even starts to get up. "It'd be like riding a surfboard."

Now I understand why Dad insists that I accompany PJ whenever he comes here to White Bay. Otherwise, he's lightened up on my having to be with PJ every single second. If Mike is with him, PJ can go in the water, even if I'm not right on the beach. Mom didn't have to worry about PJ in the waves—there aren't any. Overall, we're allowed to go pretty much wherever we want on our own as long as we announce our departure and give a return time. It's so safe here. We wear our waterproof watches and the whistles Dad gave us twenty-four hours a day.

"Sorry, PJ. No can do. Would you like someone to stand on your back and ride *you* around?"

"Maybe," he says slyly. He thinks he's being strategic. "If I liked them enough."

"Well, these turtles don't know you that well," I say. "Come on, let's go see if Mike and Dad are back yet." Mike and Dad went into town this morning and promised to bring me back some more film.

Dad's not back and Sheryl is hunched over her computer typing, so PJ and I go down to the dock to see if we can spot Bob out in the channel. Sure enough, there they are, just dropping the sails, about a quarter mile offshore. PJ hops up and down, waving, but they aren't looking our way.

As they get closer Mike ties the rubber fenders to the lifelines and tosses them over so that they hang alongside the boat to protect Bob when he's tied up against the dock. The white fenders look like giant tampons dangling off the boat, strings and all. I turn to PJ. Forget it. If Jen were here we'd have a good laugh.

About four feet from the dock, Dad tosses me a line and I loop it around the cleat once, the way I've seen Sheryl do, and pull it toward me to help straighten the boat against the dock. When it's positioned right, I tie off the line. In the meantime, Mike's jumped ashore and has cleated off the stern line. We both coil our lines in tight, flat Flemish coils so that we can walk over them on the dock without tripping. I like the way they look, all neat and nautical.

I'm busy admiring my coil when Dad shouts, "Surprise!"

He's swinging a big shopping bag from a store called Deep Blue Divers. It's not the bag, though, that grabs my attention, and it's not PJ flying past me in a mad rush to get to Dad. It's the boy climbing out of Bob's cabin, the most gorgeous boy I've ever seen in my life.

8

I'm sure glad Sheryl's not here. I know if she saw the look on my face right now her eyelid would wink itself right off her head and into the sea.

Lucky for me, Dad doesn't notice stuff like that or he'd see that my T-shirt is fluttering because my heart has gone into fifth gear. Boy, I'm so glad I didn't walk down to the dock in just my bathing suit!

Dad says, "Casey, I'd like you to meet Jonah, Anderson's nephew. Jonah, this is Casey, my oldest. PJ here is the baby."

"Da-aad!" PJ wails. He doesn't like being called a baby.

Jonah says, "Nice to meet you, Casey. I've been hearing all about you from Mike." Great, I think. Not my first choice for a PR man. I can just imagine.

I must look alarmed because then Jonah says, "Don't worry, I've got little brothers too. I know how to distinguish fact from fiction."

And what do I say? What brilliant, charming, incredibly witty thing do I say?

"Hi." That's what I say. *Hi*, in a peepy little voice that you wouldn't be at all surprised to hear coming out of the mouth of PJ's hamster.

"How come *you're* here?" PJ asks Jonah.

"I'm going to be staying here with my uncle and helping your dad set up the bird nets along Turtle Beach." Turtle Beach is a nesting beach for the sea turtles, and part of Dad's plan, besides protecting injured turtles while they heal, is to set nets up that will keep the birds, which will be waiting hungrily when the baby turtles hatch, from diving down to snack on the hatchlings. Dad figures if at least one batch of baby turtles can make it into the sea without getting eaten first, it will help swell the population. Jonah must be the muscle Dad's been wanting. And he's got it, I think, looking at his tanned, muscular arms.

All the groceries and stuff are lined up on the dock now; we each take two bags and head for the house. Jonah carries three and offers to carry one of mine.

"It's okay," I say. "Thanks."

"So how do you like our tropical paradise, Casey?" Jonah says.

"I love it," I say. The words just slip right out of my mouth, like the truth.

Now I love it, anyway, I think. Now it's looking pretty good, now that you're here and I'm not the only person here who's over ten and under forty. I sneak a quick look at him again. Damn, he's good-looking. He's lean and tall and has dark brown hair that's all one length—a little longer than is in style at home, but here, with nothing to compare him to, it looks just fine. I think about Matt and how cute he is, then I look at Jonah again. I'm not saying I'm thinking anything at all—just enjoying the sudden appearance of a boy who is not younger than me, who is not my brother and who just happens to be nice to look at. All of a sudden I feel a little less cut off from civilization.

Everybody's reading my mind today because Dad says, "Oh, Case, I've got news from the civilized world for you. This will make you happy." He hands me a postcard. From Jen! It's postmarked the day after I left California. It took more than two weeks to get here! That means my letter to her probably hasn't even reached her yet. Two weeks . . . how am I ever going to know what's going on at home? Anything—everything—can happen in two weeks.

> *Soooo, Casey . . .*
>
> *How's Paradise? Can you stand it? Shall I send the Marines?*
>
> *Hey, turn on your phone! It's not picking up. JK, I guess your mom was right about that. What a drag. :(Send smoke signals, or at least write.*
>
> *Wish you were here or that I was there!*
>
> *Love, Jen*
>
> *P.S. Matt said to say hello when I talked to you, so "Hello."*

Matt! I reach up and feel one of the earrings he gave me. I haven't taken them off once. I try to imagine where Matt is right now and what he's doing. I completely forget Jonah walking beside me until he speaks up in a way that makes me realize he's repeating something he just said and that I didn't hear.

"Mike said you're a good photographer."

For a second I'm confused, half-expecting to have to deny whatever it is Mike said about me—did Jonah really say "good"? A compliment, from Mike?

"Well, I took a thirty-five-millimeter class last semester and really enjoyed it," I say, still feeling unsure. "In fact, I've already used up all my film."

"I happen to know that your dad picked up a few rolls for you," Jonah says, rattling one of the grocery bags. "He said you were good too."

Good. Well, there it is!

At the house we put the stuff away in the kitchen. Sheryl is making lunch. She says, "I saw you arrive and figured you'd be hungry. I hope you didn't eat in town."

"No," Dad says, "Mike was too eager to get back here with the presents." He hugs Sheryl and kisses her on the neck. It's nice, really, the way they are with each other, even if it is a little embarrassing sometimes. They never fight, not like he and Mom used to when they were married.

"What presents?" I ask.

"That's the surprise," Dad says. He picks up the Deep Blue Diver bag and peers into it with a puzzled look on his face, the way he used to on Christmas morning. He'd stare at the name tags on presents for a long time, acting confused, as if he didn't know who each package was for. When I was little, it drove me nuts, which was the whole point, of course. Now I have mature patience. And I have PJ.

PJ doesn't have an ounce of mature patience; he jumps up and down, wanting to know what's in the bag. This allows me to maintain my aloof composure in front of Jonah.

Dad reaches into the bag and pulls out face masks, then fins, then snorkels. "Blue for Casey, green for PJ and these are Mike's."

It's obvious Mike picked out his own because they're completely black. Mr. Cool. Actually, they do look pretty cool—kind of like Darth Vader meets Jacques Cousteau.

"Awesome!" PJ says, his face already in his mask. He sounds like he's talking from inside a phone booth.

"Do you even know what it's for, PJ?" Mike says. Mr. Expert.

"You don't put your mouth in it, just your eyes and nose, or else you won't be able to breathe." Mike hooks PJ's snorkel up to the mask strap and sticks it in PJ's mouth.

PJ runs around the kitchen breathing in and out of it loudly and shouting "Toot! Toot!" through his snorkel. What a goofball.

Jonah says, "After lunch I'll get my gear and we can snorkel at Mahoe. That's the best spot."

"Sure," I say. I don't know where Mahoe is and I don't care. It sounds great to me. Besides, I'm glad he's joining us for lunch. My head is still whirling at this new development. A new person, someone my age, someone to talk to, maybe be friends with, maybe . . . maybe what? No, not going there. What am I thinking, I don't even know yet if we're going to get along well enough to be friends, let alone anything else that I am not actually even thinking about. No, not me. I reach up and touch one of my dangling dolphins.

"What's snorkel?" PJ wants to know.

"You'll see," we all say, not just Dad.

I know that PJ's going to love this. I remember having a mask and snorkel when Mom and Dad were still married and we lived in a bigger house, with a pool. I'd scatter nickels all over the bottom of the pool and go looking for them with my mask and snorkel on. I'd stay in the pool until my skin pruned up and by the time I got out I'd have a mask ring on my face that would last through dinner.

After lunch Sheryl shoos us out, saying she'll clean up. I don't look at her so I miss the wink. She might be old, but she's not blind, and I know she knows Jonah's awfully good-looking and that I've certainly noticed. Sometimes when she and I have been in the kitchen alone together, talking, she's asked me about my life and friends at home. I haven't said too much about Matt, but when I have mentioned him, she's smiled knowingly at me, as if she understands perfectly what it's like, as if she were my age, or remembered really well being my age, and knows how it is to like someone. I feel as if I could talk to her more like a friend than I could my mom. Maybe it's because she seems closer to my age than she does a full-on grown-up parent type. That could just be because of the way she looks: with her short hair, trail shorts and tank tops she doesn't seem anything like my mom, who's always dressed pretty nice. Or maybe it's just because she isn't my mom, or anyone else's mom for that matter.

I have this feeling that right now she's probably thinking I might like Jonah. Not that I don't. Not that I do!

We head over to Mahoe Bay, which turns out to be the

beach on the farthest side of the island, the one the boys have named Lizard Beach, since it's directly across from Lizard Island.

Personally, this is one of my favorite spots. When I've been free of Mike and PJ for a little while I've liked coming here by myself just to think. I'm sure I've already done enough thinking, though, to last me halfway through the tenth grade. I'm ready for a distraction. I glance at Jonah. He's distracting.

PJ says, "Hey, this is Lizard Beach. We already discovered this beach last week."

"Lizard? Huh. Well, I must be mistaken," Jonah says. "I probably saw the name on a really old map." He smiles at me and shrugs with a question-mark look on his face.

"They've named all the beaches and half the plants," I explain, indicating Mike and PJ, who have plopped down on the sand and are undoing their sandals.

"How old is PJ?"

"He's seven. Mike is ten." I almost start to tell him that I'm fourteen and a half, then stop myself.

"Hey, I have a seven-year-old brother," Jonah says. "Also twin brothers who're five."

"I thought two brothers was a lot."

"I've got a little sister, too, Annie. She's eight. Or, I guess I should say eight and a *half*, since that half seems to be pretty important to her lately."

"Do you have any older brothers and sisters?" I ask.

"No, I'm the oldest. I just turned sixteen . . . then there was a big gap between me and my sister."

"I'm the oldest too," I say. I think I'll just leave it at that.

From his gear bag Jonah pulls a travel-size tube of Crest toothpaste. He squeezes some out on each of our fingertips and tells us to coat the inside glass of our face masks with it, then rinse out the masks in the sea.

"I guess we won't have to worry about nasal cavities, huh?" I say. That's something Matt would have said. It just popped into my brain and right out of my mouth. Now I feel like a dork.

Jonah laughs. "Yeah, it helps control tartar buildup too." That makes me feel a little better.

"Eewwww! That's boogers!" Mike says, Mr. Disgusting. That doesn't make me feel better.

"The toothpaste will break the surface tension of the water on your masks and keep them from fogging up," Jonah says. "Spit works too, but you've got to have the right kind."

"Like a loogie?" Mike says. Mr. Class.

"Something like that," Jonah says. "Okay, PJ, all set?"

PJ nods and answers a distant "Ready" through his snorkel. I want to laugh, looking at Mike and PJ with their face masks on and their faces pressed flat like they're in a wind tunnel, but then I realize that I must look as ridiculous as they do.

Jonah leads PJ into the water until he's waist-deep, then hands him his fins. Mike and I follow, putting our fins on after we're a few feet into the water. We'd fall on our butts if we tried to do it onshore.

"All set?"

"Ready!" we say in a chorus of hollow voices that sound as if they're coming from inside a drainpipe.

We plunge, facefirst, into the water. PJ is out in a hot minute, choking on the water in his snorkel and trying to hop up and down, which doesn't quite work since he's now shoulder-deep in the ocean.

"What's wrong?"

"Fish!" he says. "There's lots of fish in there. They'll bite my toes!"

Jonah steadies PJ and tips his snorkel to drain out the water. "PJ, remember what I told you. If you get water in the snorkel, just blow into it. Hard." PJ does it. "Great. Now, as for the fish, they're a lot more scared of you than you are of them. Just try to touch one."

PJ sticks his head in the water again. We all watch underwater as a small yellow-and-black-striped fish comes right at him. PJ bravely holds his ground and when the fish seems like it's close enough to touch, PJ reaches for it. The fish is gone. Zoom, out of sight, gone. PJ pops his head up.

"What was it?" He is gleeful at his power. I feel really grateful to Jonah for being so nice to PJ and for knowing just what to say. There's something so appealing about seeing guys be nice to little kids.

It occurs to me that Patty Harper is probably thinking the same thing, maybe even right this minute, watching Matt be nice to the little kids on the playground. That thought makes my stomach feel like it's twisting around inside my body.

"That was a sergeant major," Jonah says. "You'll see lots of those, they're about the most common fish here. They're the pigeons of the sea."

Jonah has pushed his mask on top of his head. With his hair slicked back he looks even older than sixteen. And very cute.

I, on the other hand, already know that I look totally stupid when my hair is wet and slicked back. Everytime I get out of the shower and clear the fog off the mirror I see myself and think that I look about twelve and could use a pound of mascara. I immediately stick my face back in the water and swim away.

I'm amazed at what I am seeing. Fish everywhere. There are swaying purple sea fans; orange, green and red sponges; some kind of underwater lettucelike plants with frilly deep green leaves; and little shells clinging to them here and there. I can't believe I've been swimming in this water every day without once thinking about what was *in* it. And there sure is a lot in it.

Jonah leads us to the edge of the bay where plants and coral grow, forming a reef. We snorkel along slowly out to the point. Because we're breathing the whole time and mostly just floating on our stomachs, it doesn't take any effort at all to swim a long way offshore. Wearing fins is like having little outboard motors on your feet. A quick flip of your foot propels you forward. It's nothing like normal swimming, where you have to keep moving your arms and legs and alternate between holding your breath and gulping in air.

Every now and then Jonah points something out, sticking his head above water to tell us what it is. Even with our faces in the water, our ears are mostly exposed, so we can hear Jonah without having to take our eyes off whatever he's describing.

The fat fish, brightly decorated in green, blue and yellow, like parrots, are called parrotfish. Jonah tells us that the really pretty ones are the males and the dull ones are the females. He says that if there aren't enough females, some will change sex. When Jonah tells us this I feel embarrassed in every direction. First, because he's talking about fish sex. Then because I'm waiting either for PJ to pipe up with a bunch of questions or for Mike to make a stupid joke. Luckily, a large school of yellowtail damselfish swims by and Jonah starts talking about them.

I think the damselfish are my favorite. They have blue-black bodies with tiny bright, fluorescent stars on them and, of course, yellow tails.

"That long skinny fish hanging in that plant there? That's a trumpetfish," Jonah says. Finally! A fish that's not named for how it looks. It doesn't look anything like a trumpet—more like a legless horse standing on its tail. I guess that wouldn't be a great name.

"Watch him change color," Jonah says. Sure enough, as soon as Jonah waves his hand at it the trumpetfish turns from brown to bright yellow with a blue head! Camouflage, Jonah tells us. Camouflage is big here underwater. Jonah points out some small, flat white fish that look like the ends of peacock feathers with large black circles at their tails. He says the circle is meant to look like the fish's eye so that other fish will go after the wrong end, and the peacock fish can get away by shooting off in a direction that his predator wasn't expecting him to go.

"What's that fish on the rock that looks like a lizard?" I ask, scaring it off. Its colors change too, from brown to pale green, as it passes over different rocks and plants on the bottom.

"A lizardfish," Jonah says. So, basically, it's a lizard with gills. Great, we really needed some more lizards around here because one hundred land species just aren't enough.

Jonah identifies all the coral for us. Star coral has star-shaped patterns all over. Brain coral is the color of split-pea soup and looks just like a brain, with a maze of ridges. There are huge domes of brain coral just beneath us, in about ten feet of water. Jonah says that when it's this big, it's over a hundred years old.

"See that mustard-colored stuff growing over there?" We all nod underwater. "That's fire coral. Watch out for it. It really burns if you touch it. Really, you shouldn't touch *any-thing* down here. The bacteria on your fingers is death to the coral. Everywhere a human touches it, it dies. It takes years for it to grow, but just a few seconds to be destroyed."

A lot sure can happen in a short time. Show up at the dock to carry groceries and meet a nice guy. Stick your face in the water and you're in a whole 'nother world.

"Keep your eyes open," Jonah says. "The more slowly you move through the water the more you'll see. You have to fight that urge to keep moving and get to the next rock or plant. You'll miss a lot of good stuff that way. A bunch of fish disappear when you first arrive, but they'll come back if you stay still, wait and watch."

I'm trying not to miss anything, to stay still and take his advice, but the truth is, I'm watching Jonah more than the fish.

9

All week, Dad's kept Jonah busy helping him construct frames for the nets they're putting up at Turtle Beach. If they finish early, Jonah will usually come find my brothers and me and take a swim with us, or sit and talk with me on the beach while we watch them play in the water. He tells me all kinds of stuff about the sea life and the birds here. I can tell he really cares about this environment, and he's making me appreciate what a special place this is. He plans to study marine biology in college. He never gets tired of talking about the island and I never get tired of hearing him talk about it.

A few days ago we were sitting on the sand, looking at the water, not talking, just enjoying the view, when Jonah said, "Have you seen the wink yet?"

For a minute I thought he was talking about Sheryl.

"Right at sunset, just when the last little edge of the sun

drops behind the horizon there's a green wink. They call it the green flash."

"I have a feeling you're just teasing me," I said.

"No, really, it's true," he said. "I've actually seen it a few times. Some people never see it, though." We watched the sun go down, but there was no wink. Jonah said, "It's really hard to catch and maybe it doesn't happen every single sunset."

I've been trying to catch it, but I haven't. I still thought he might be teasing me, but this morning Dad and Sheryl backed him up.

Dad really likes Jonah. So does PJ, and Mike for that matter. And me, of course.

Yesterday, Sheryl said to me, "It sure is nice [wink, wink] that you and Jonah are getting along so well. I'm glad you've found someone your age to play with." Like I'd been having a hard time finding anyone up until now, like there was even anyone to choose from.

Anyway, *play* is not the word I'd think of for someone my age. I mean, I stopped *playing* when I was about ten. Then I moved on to . . . *hanging around*. But that's okay; I know what she means. And it's true, I'm glad to have someone here who's my age, whatever we're doing.

Today Sheryl and I have been sitting on the terrace since lunch, enjoying the view and the tradewinds, which kick up in the afternoons.

She's working on a report and I'm reading a book Jen gave me, called *I'm Kissing as Fast as I Can*. Well, I'm sort of reading it. It's hard to keep my attention focused on my book with one eye on the water (it's impossible not to look at it every other minute, it's so incredibly beautiful), and one eye on the path between here and Anderson's house, where Jonah is staying. That doesn't leave an eye for this book.

I'm hoping Dad will finish early today so Jonah and I (and unfortunately Mike and PJ) can go to Mahoe again. All week I've been wanting to get over there and snorkel again, but I've been waiting, hoping Jonah will come. Waiting for him makes me feel like my mom, who's afraid to go out and miss a phone call. I probably should have just gone over there on my own; it's not like Jonah would have any trouble finding me. When Jonah does show up, there won't be any way of avoiding taking Mike and PJ with us because as soon as they see we're going, they'll run and get their gear. Besides, Jonah will invite them, I know.

While I've been sitting here, my head snapping back and forth between the sea and the path like I'm at a tennis game or something, I've also been sneaking peeks at my legs. I can't help noticing that I've started to look pretty good. A weird thing to say, but since I'm only *thinking* it, who'll know?

For one, I'm getting a nice, even tan. This will probably haunt me when I'm old. They say in your thirties you pay for the sun you got in your teens. It's not like I'm *trying* to get a tan or anything. Around here I can't help it; it just happens. I've been wearing sunscreen. Number fifteen.

Plus, I'm getting muscles! I think it's all the hiking, carting stuff around and swimming. I'm not buff or anything, just starting to look athletic, like Sheryl. I like the way it looks and the way it makes me feel, like I'm strong.

The other thing that's happened is the sun is lightening my hair and I'm getting blond streaks mixed in with my normally boring brown hair. It looks like I paid to have it done. And my hair has fluffed up, too, like a duck's feathers, but not in a bad way. I mean, it's softer and fuller. It must be the clean air and all the salt water. The smog at home must weigh my hair down. Too bad I can't mix it up a little. The air from here, my friends from home . . . a telephone!

But if I had a phone, be it tele or cell, I'd probably be calling Jen three times a day, telling her every little thing that's going on and every word that Jonah's said to me plus giving her a head-to-toe description of him. As it is, it's getting harder and harder to imagine Jen and Matt and everyone, and what they might be doing. They all seem very far away.

Yesterday morning I rode into town with Dad just so I could see if there was any mail for me at the post office. Just a short note from Mom saying she's having a great time and hopes we're wearing sunscreen and being careful. Jeez. Seeing her handwriting, though, made me miss her and want to talk to her so I used Dad's calling card and the pay phone in town.

"Hi, Mom."

"Casey! What a surprise. It's nice to hear your voice."

"You too, Mom. How's your vacation going? Are you enjoying all the peace and quiet without us kids around?"

"It hasn't been that quiet. We had a record month at the office so we're planning a little fiesta at Casa Teresita this weekend and I'm in charge of putting that together. I'm going to bring Roger; this will be the first time I've actually brought him to any office event. . . ."

She sounded really happy and her usual hyper self. While she was talking I found myself watching a pelican in the bay across from where I was standing at the pay phone. A sea-gull had landed right on its head; it looked ridiculous. I don't realize how big the pelicans are until I see them next to the gulls, which are fairly good-sized birds themselves. The gulls are scavengers and when the pelicans are fishing, the seagulls like to hang around (and sometimes just perch right on top of) the pelicans to pick up any scraps or left-overs from their catches. The pelicans don't even seem to notice when they've got a big seagull perched on their backs or even on the tops of their heads.

Mom was still talking and I guiltily put the phone back to my ear. I hadn't even realized that I'd been kind of hold-ing it away from me, not so I couldn't hear her, just so her voice would be quieted a bit. It's just so not noisy here on the islands, and the way she was talking and what she was talking about just didn't fit in with what I was experiencing around me. The pace of this place is so different from the world on the other end of that telephone line.

"Mom, that sounds great," I said, when it seemed like the right time to throw that in. "I'm glad you had a good month. I'm sure you'll do a perfect job with the party, you al-ways do."

She asked how we were doing and I told her a little about how pretty the water was and how we'd been sailing and hiking. "I should go, though, Mom. It's really expensive to call and Dad's waiting for me so we can get back to the island."

"Okay, honey. It was good to talk to you. Give PJ and Mike big kisses for me."

"Mike won't let me, but I'll give PJ two really big sloppy ones."

I had thought I would splurge and call Jen right afterward, just for a quick hello, but after talking to Mom I decided I didn't want to have that hectic, electronic world intruding on my state of mind.

Thinking about that now makes me feel so bad, well, guilty, mostly. Guilty that I felt impatient on the phone with Mom. After all, I've spent all kinds of time talking with Sheryl about sea turtles and coral—two things I never cared about before, or even knew about for that matter. And guilty that I haven't been doing much letter writing. I decide to write Jen a letter, even though I can't mail it today.

Just as I get up to find some paper (and take my hundredth look up the path) PJ bursts through the trees.

"Casey! Casey! We undid a turtle!"

My mind fast-forwards through all the possibilities. *Undid?* That doesn't sound good.

"What are you talking about, PJ?"

PJ's huffing and puffing, bending over his knees, catching his breath. His hair is sticking straight up. His cheeks are bright red.

"They had to put a rope in the water to get him out. They saved him."

"PJ, calm down a second and tell me what you're talking about. What do you mean, they 'undid' a turtle?"

"It got stuck, under a ledge, a rock, you know, *underwater*, and he wouldn't be able to breathe down there forever. They can only stay under for forty minutes, you know. And they can't swim backwards. Jonah and Dad took turns diving to get him out, but they couldn't budge him, so they had to tie a rope around him. Dad had to use a tank to breathe and then they looped a rope around his shell and then they pulled the turtle out backwards but he got away before they could untie him so Jonah had to go after him and cut the rope, so the turtle wouldn't swim away with a rope around him and get caught again. They saved him! You should have seen Dad and Jonah down there in all the bubbles."

While PJ's coming up for air himself, Dad and Jonah come along down the trail. They're both dripping wet.

"Hi, Sheryl, Casey," Jonah says when he reaches the house and drops his gear on the porch steps. "I guess PJ told you about our little rescue mission."

Sheryl and I nod. Dad drops his gear beside Jonah's and sits down next to Sheryl.

Jonah says, "PJ was pretty funny. The whole time we were trying to unjam the turtle, he was hopping from one foot to the other. He couldn't decide whether he wanted to stay and watch us or run and get you so you could watch too. He didn't want you to miss anything exciting."

"Sounds like I missed a lot," I say.

Jonah stands next to me and kind of whispers in my ear, "Nah. PJ was the most exciting thing going. We just popped a turtle out from under an overhanging rock ledge. We've had to do it before. No big deal, really."

His voice against my new duck hair is making my skin tingle. I'm really grateful for this tan now because I'm sure I'm blushing. I refuse to even look in Sheryl's direction.

Finally I say, "What bubbles was he talking about, the turtle's?"

Jonah laughs. Dad chimes in. "Air bubbles, from the scuba tanks. We put on our gear to go down into the pen. Jonah brought the tanks over this morning from town. We haven't had them for two weeks because they've been in for inspection. I'm sure glad we had them today."

Jonah must have taken the Whaler, our only means of transportation, besides Bob and our feet. The Whaler is a powerboat that goes a lot faster than Bob. Bob has to tack back and forth in a zigzag pattern to catch the wind. It takes more than an hour to get across in Bob, even though it's only four miles. The Whaler just rips straight across the channel in about fifteen minutes.

"In fact," Dad says, "Jonah and I thought you might really enjoy scuba diving. While you're here you might like to get certified. What do you think?"

I think, how come my dad and Jonah are talking about me in this chummy way? I wonder what else Jonah's been talking to Dad about?

"I don't know," I say. "What would I have to do?" I like swimming, I'm thinking, but there are an awful lot of creatures down there. Breathing underwater . . . I don't know. I feel as if I've pushed the limits of my bravery already: snorkeling, swimming in the ocean, sailing across the channel, flying here in a little plane, going to bed knowing there are lizards lurking in every tree and bush—maybe even under my bed.

"Well," Jonah says, "there's a textbook you'll have to read first. You can borrow mine. Your dad and I can teach you about the equipment. All the guys at Deep Blue Divers are instructors; they would take you in the water. We can talk to them. You could probably get certified in a couple of weeks."

"Is that like having a driver's license to go underwater?" PJ asks.

"Sort of."

"Can I do it too?"

"Sorry, kiddo," Dad says, "you've got to be at least twelve. I'm afraid that leaves you and Mike out."

Finally! Something I could do without those two tagging along. Every minute that Jonah's been around, so have my little brothers. Especially PJ. In fact, I think PJ is in love. I feel as if I'm competing with PJ for Jonah's attention. Not that *I'm* in love or anything. Just trying to have a little quality time with someone my own age. Right. I mean, I *think* that's all it is. But I sure have found myself thinking about Jonah a lot lately.

"Well," I say, finally. "Maybe. I'll have to think about it." I'm trying to sound a lot more nonchalant than I feel. I want Jonah to think I'm adventurous and not afraid of anything. I want my mind to catch up with my new muscles. I wish I could just say, "Sure! Sounds great!" I'm sure that's what Jen would do. Only, if I were Jen, I would have thought of it myself and would be begging them to teach me.

Jonah says, "We're done for the day. Anyone interested in going to Mahoe?"

Dad says he's got paperwork to do. That's one down.

Mike's on the beach in front of the house. He's totally engrossed in building an enormous fort out of sand and seashells. That's two.

Sheryl's nodding off in the hammock (three!), so Jonah and I head over toward Mahoe Bay, PJ trailing behind us. (Three out of four isn't bad.) I suppose it wouldn't be very nice to wish for a small patch of quicksand to appear, about three feet deep, perfect for PJ. Nothing permanent, just enough for him to sink in up to his neck for a couple of hours.

About halfway to Mahoe, Jonah says, "Hey, would you guys like to go over to Lizard Island instead?"

"You mean swim over?" PJ says. The little island really does look as if you could swim to it, but once we got into the channel between the islands it would get pretty rough, even if we were wearing our fins and snorkels.

"No, I was thinking of Bob. Let's go back."

I haven't really wanted to go over there, particularly given the island's name and all, but I'm happy to be spending this time with Jonah, so I just smile and nod. As I start to do an about-face in the direction of the dock, I get a flash of my mom jetting down the hall to catch the phone. But I like Jonah, I think. I want to spend this time with him; it'll be fun. I suppose it's not really fair to assume that my mom doesn't think the same thing when she's heading out the door with Roger. I look out to the sea and then up at the blue sky, glad that I'm here and not having to choose golf.

While Jonah goes to the house to tell Dad we're taking Bob, PJ and I go down to the dock to ready the boat.

"Casey, I've been thinking about the turtle that got stuck."

"Yeah, PJ?" I say, loading our stuff into the lockers under the seats in Bob's cockpit. "What about it?"

"Well, do you think he was trying to kill himself?"

"PJ! What made you think of that? How do you even know about stuff like that?"

"I saw this movie once, on TV? And this lady stuck her head in the oven and tried to kill herself."

Great. I'm actually starting to agree with all those grown-ups who complain about what kids see on television.

"You know you're not supposed to be watching those kinds of shows, Mom said."

"I wasn't! It was a comedy, honest. The lady didn't die."

"Okay, okay. So how does this relate to the turtle?"

"Well," PJ says, scrunching his forehead up. "I was just thinking, it's like he was trying to stick his head in the oven, too. Like he was saying, 'Goodbye, cruel world.' "

Goodbye, cruel world? From now on I'm monitoring everything this kid watches.

"I don't think so, PJ. That's not the kind of thing I think turtles think about. Besides, why would a *turtle* feel that way?"

"Well, turtles are alive, you know."

Oh, right, I forgot, like hamsters and seagulls. Aliveness is really a big thing to my little brother, the existentialist.

"I mean," PJ goes on, "they have feelings too, you know.

Maybe the turtle is sad because he's stuck in the pen and he can't go swimming in the ocean with his friends. Maybe he just wants to go home but he can't get out because Dad's got him trapped."

"PJ, you know Dad's not trying to hurt the turtles, don't you?"

PJ nods, but he doesn't look convinced.

"Dad's trying to *help* them. The pen isn't a trap. You know they're only in there if they're sick or have been hurt, right? Dad measures and tags them, and when they're okay, he lets them go."

"I know, but *they* don't know why they're there," PJ says.

He has a point. That's the hardest part about animals. You can't explain anything to them.

"Well, I know you can't tell the turtles, but don't you think they figure it out after a while? I mean, since no one is hurting them, and they get fed and in a few weeks they get let out and go back to their friends?"

"I guess."

"What happened to the turtle that Dad and Jonah rescued this morning? Didn't you say he took off?"

"That's how Dad found him. Dad went in the water to open the gate to the pen. They were going to let that turtle and another one out today anyway."

"See?" I say, hoping that settles the discussion. Where's Jonah anyway? Hanging around with PJ is making me depressed.

Finally Jonah comes trotting down the path from the house. "Ready, mates?" he says. "PJ, want to take the helm while we shove you off?"

"Only if someone stays in the boat with me," PJ says.

"Afraid we won't get on the boat in time?" Jonah laughs, stepping onto the side deck. He uncleats the main halyard, which we'll use to raise the mainsail. Since we've been here, Dad has taken us out on a couple of sails to show us the island from offshore. I'm feeling secretly proud of myself that I'm getting to know what most of the stuff on the boat is called. I even know what a lot of it does.

Thinking I'll get a jump on things before Jonah has to tell me what to do, I untie the docklines. Then I hop into the cockpit and sit next to PJ, who's got his hand on the tiller ready to go. I lean over the side of the boat and push us away from the dock.

I'm still feeling pretty proud of myself as the boat begins drifting away from the dock. Jonah looks around when he notices that the boat has started moving. He looks surprised but he doesn't say anything.

Then I realize: "The motor! We didn't start the motor! What's going to happen?"

"Since it's not windy, not much. Luckily," Jonah says. "Next time, though, you might want to wait until either the sail is up or the motor is on before you untie the boat from the dock, otherwise you're just adrift with no control over the boat."

Oops.

Jonah loosens the ties on the folded mainsail, then uses the halyard to raise the sail. He tells me to keep the boat pointed into the wind so that the sail doesn't fill up with wind. The sail flaps like mad and makes a huge racket but I know it's okay, even though it makes my heart race.

"Go ahead and fall off," Jonah says once he's raised the sail to the top of the mast. Without hesitating or trying to remember which side is which, I push the tiller to starboard.

Jonah climbs into the cockpit and takes hold of the mainsheet, which controls the mainsail. When he sits down next to me I notice that my heart cranks up again. What is happening here? As if I don't know, as if I'm two people and only one of me knows—or will admit—that it's Jonah and not the luffing sails that is making my heart skip beats.

10

Once we're underway, with both sails up, PJ abandons his pretend stint at the tiller and goes forward to sit on the bow. It's really hard to keep from saying, "Be careful. Hang on to the lifeline. Don't fall overboard," like Mom would. I notice Dad doesn't say stuff like that to us ever. Neither does Sheryl.

"Go ahead and kick back for a while," Jonah says. "I'll take the tiller until we tack."

I sit on the starboard side lazaret, the seat in the cockpit, with my back to the cabin and my perfectly tanned legs out in front of me, hoping Jonah will notice. It would be nice if I had a little cleavage to go with them. I look down at my chest. No startling developments there. My legs look great, though, except for a few mosquito bites. I point my toes.

"Oh, I almost forgot," Jonah says. "When I went for the tanks this morning, I picked up your family's mail. Your dad was going through it just now when I asked him if we could take Bob. Here, he gave me this to give to you." Jonah pulls a letter from the pocket of his shorts and hands it to me.

It's from Matt.

Matt! I'm so glad it's not a postcard that everyone else would have read by now. As it is, the envelope looks pretty beat up.

I turn it over a couple of times, reading the postmark, the return address, his name, my name. I like the way Matt writes my name, all in caps in his boxy printing.

"Aren't you going to read it?" Jonah says, not looking at me, looking straight ahead to Lizard Island.

"I'll wait," I say.

Jonah gives me a funny, knowing smile that makes me think he thinks he's a lot more than just a year and a half older than me.

Even though I don't want to open the letter in front of Jonah, when I stick it in the outside pocket of the blue bag Jen gave me, I feel guilty, as if I'm hiding Matt. It's bad enough that lately I've been thinking about him less and less and thinking about Jonah more and more.

"We need to tack," Jonah says. "Take the tiller."

"I'll work the jib sheets," I say. I say this as if I always do the sheets. Mike does it, I think. Sheryl does it. I never do it.

"Sure," Jonah says. "Ready about!"

I'm not ready!

I'm still sitting, showing off my legs, but I answer, "Ready!" and jump up. I grab the jib sheet but realize I'm not really ready and when Jonah turns the boat and the sail crosses over the bow, the wind yanks the sheet right out of my hands. It flies out over the side of the boat. I barely have time to grab it before it completely unwinds itself from the winch. I start pulling like crazy; it takes a lot of grunting (not very alluring, I'm sure) for me to haul the sheet in and start winding it around the winch. Jonah, who sees what is happening, turns the boat back into the wind and takes the pressure off the sails for me.

I manage to cleat off the jib sheet, pull the other one back into the cockpit before I fall onto the lazaret sweating.

"You've got that sail in pretty tight," Jonah says. "Want to let it out a bit?"

"Sure," I say, but hesitate because now I'm afraid it will fly out of my hands again and Jonah will think I'm totally useless.

"Here," Jonah says. "Put your palm against the wraps on the winch, like this." He takes my hand and lays it against the sheet wrapped around the winch. Then he puts his hand over mine.

"Now, use this hand as a brake against the winch. Good, not too much, you'll end up having to trim it in again." His hand on mine is very distracting. His whole body leaning over me is even more distracting. I wish my neck weren't so sweaty.

I inch the sheet out a little at a time until he says, "That's it, perfect." He leans against the stern rail. "We'll be there in a few minutes. Why don't you take the helm when I drop the sails?" he says.

"Good idea," I say. "Since I'm obviously such an expert sailor."

"You did okay," he says, giving me a big smile.

* * *

From here at the shoreline of Lizard Island, our island, Ginger, looks completely different. I've seen it coming across the channel from Tartuga, but from this angle it's a lot hillier than I'd realized. To think I've been hiking over it almost every day! No wonder I'm getting so strong.

After we anchor Bob in the little bay that faces Mahoe on Ginger, we pile ourselves and our gear into the dinghy and motor ashore. We have to pull the dinghy right up onto the beach and tie its anchor line around a tree. This doesn't seem very nautical to me, but Jonah says that's how it's done.

"So," I say, looking at all the footpaths that lead away from the beach and into the interior of the island, "exactly why do they call this Lizard Island?"

"Beats me," Jonah says. "A lot of times they name islands because of their shape, like West Dog. From a distance it kind of looks like a sleeping dog. Anguilla's named because it's shaped like an eel. Virgin Gorda, which you can't see from here, is the fattest of the Virgin Islands."

"What's a virgin?" PJ asks.

"PJ, why don't you get our stuff out of the dinghy and put it under that tree, out of the sun," I say, blushing.

At the head of one of the footpaths, I peer into the shady interior. The paths are like tunnels because of the way the trees meet overhead. The sea grape trees on these islands aren't tall; they spread out more than grow up. Their leaves are bright green and round, not pointed like most trees, and the bark is dark, almost black.

Something in the tree moves. Leaping lizards! I jump

backward. Jonah is standing right behind me and I slam into him.

"Sorry," he says, "didn't mean to scare you. Mosquito?"

"Oh, I don't know, something just startled me," I say.

"Why don't we hike through? This trail makes a nice circle through the island and lands right back over there. We can swim when we get back. We'll be nice and sweaty."

Great. Like I'm not already dripping buckets of salt water from every conceivable surface on my body. Fifteen feet away from the water, the breeze disappears and the sweat starts pouring. Very attractive.

All our clothes have interesting white patterns in them from the salt in our sweat. My T-shirts, even after they've been washed and hung in the sun to dry, feel swollen and vaguely damp, as if the salt particles trapped in the fabric are drinking up the moisture in the air. I don't mind this effect on my hair, but I miss putting on a shirt that feels totally clean and dry.

We start along the trail, PJ in front. Every few feet I hear scuffling in the brush and under the leaves that cover the ground. Lizards, I just know it. Trillions of them. Every variety. If it weren't for wanting to be with Jonah, I'm sure I'd live a happy life without ever having set foot on Lizard Island.

"Look!" PJ says. He's squatting down to peer at something on the ground. Oh God, I hope he hasn't picked up a lizard. I'm imagining it dangling from his thumb, like the ones hanging from that woman's earlobes at the airport. I shut my eyes.

"Hold out your hand," Jonah says. *Oh no.* I open my eyes to see him place a black-and-white-speckled shell the size and shape of a snail in PJ's open hand. PJ holds very still.

"Shhh," Jonah says. "Just wait."

In a minute, two purple claws that seem too big to fit in the shell peek out and unfold, then some antennae, then part of the orange body of a crab. When its legs are unfolded and sticking out of its shell, the crab takes two tentative steps across PJ's palm, wobbling under the weight of its shell. PJ giggles, and the crab snaps back into its shell really fast. We stand there while PJ goes through this about five hundred more times.

The crab never makes it more than a step or two across PJ's palm before PJ's giggling sends it back inside for cover.

"PJ, hold still. You're scaring him," I say.

"It tickles! *You* try it."

I take the crab, reluctantly—it makes me think of a bug or a spider—and rest it on my open palm. When his tiny claws poke out, I try to freeze but I can't—it tickles! The crab ducks back into his shell.

"Do you think we should take him back to the water?" I ask hopefully, thinking longingly of the beach, where there's a breeze and where there aren't a hundred million different kinds of lizards slithering around.

"These guys don't live in the water," Jonah says. "Look around."

I do. Then I see them. Everywhere. Scrabbling along in the sandy earth, crossing the path behind us, flipping leaves over as they scurry along. They're in the trees, too. The trees!

Funny how I didn't notice them until I stopped and my

eyes adjusted to the scenery. They just sort of came into view then. Like the reef fish. It's the same thing. When I first stick my face in the water and look around I don't see much, just a lot of sergeant majors and parrotfish. But then, if I hover in one spot, without moving, other fish and things start appearing, as if out of thin air—or water. There'll be creatures everywhere. There are cleaner shrimp and inch-long silver-and-black gobies, which hang out on rocks waiting for bigger fish to pull up. Then the gobies swim into their mouths and around their gills and scour off all the bacteria and stuff that collects there. There are tiny green crabs that munch away at the furry growth on the rocks; brightly colored sea slugs that look like frilly lettuce; almost invisible neon shrimp with incredibly long feelers that hide inside purple vase sponges, and all kinds of little creatures that pop their heads up through the little holes and openings in the coral heads.

The best is the squid. I never notice them right away. Then I get this feeling, like something is watching me. Then I see them—big eyes, iridescent spots, really weird-looking. They are about as long as my foot and can swim backward or forward, whichever way they need to go to get away from me. They shoot water through their bodies to propel themselves along, changing colors as they go. But they can also be translucent, which is why I don't notice them right away.

PJ is racing around, talking to all the little crabs. He's in heaven.

Jonah says, "Hadn't you noticed all the noise? That's these guys cruising around."

I look at him, surprised. I'm so happy.

"What did you think the noise was?" he asks when he sees the relief on my face.

"Oh, nothing."

We follow the path through to the other side of the island. From a rocky perch on a low cliff we take in the view. There are no beaches on this side of the island.

We head back, single file, PJ way up ahead of us, leading the way with a long stick he's picked up.

When PJ reaches the beach he calls back to me, "I'm going to get my snorkel and stuff and put it on."

"Okay," I yell back. "Don't go in the water until we get there."

"I know!" he says, sounding a little exasperated with me.

It takes him forever anyway, to get his mask toothpasted and the straps untwisted from the last time he went in. He disappears into the bright sunlight.

The vegetation on these islands is so thick that once you're off the beach, it's shady, almost dark compared to the glaring sunlight out on the sand. But it's not cool. It's humid and close, like a Laundromat.

I stop for a moment to take it all in (and wipe the sweat off my face with my T-shirt). I'm on a completely deserted island.

Suddenly I'm glad I've been incommunicado on this trip. Not having some electronic device beeping and flashing at me all the time has been freeing. It's made me slow down and look around, like we need to do when we're snorkeling if we don't want to miss stuff. I feel as if I'm really *here*, right where I am, right *now*, instead of always having some part of my mind occupied with another place, waiting for a message or thinking about what I'm going to say.

Do I *really* wish I were home? Or that Jen and Matt were here? We'd have a great time, I'm sure.

Jonah stops next to me. "It's nice, huh?"

I look around. I can see the incredible turquoise of the sea through the natural frame of the trees; the path we've been traveling on is white sand, as if we've never left the beach; the background music is the sound of birds and purple and orange crabs going about their business at my feet—and lizards, too, I suppose.

"Yes," I say. "It's *very* nice."

"Like you," Jonah says, and kisses me.

11

Well, *that* answers a few questions! Like, has Jonah even noticed that I'm a girl and not just an older, taller version of PJ?

(Yes!)

And, wasn't I kind of hoping what just happened would happen?

(Okay, yes.)

And, do I *really* wish Jen were here?

(Not right this minute.)

Or Matt?

(Um, no.)

"Cayyyyseeee!" PJ howls.

Then we hear it. Rain. Because of the canopy of leaves over our heads, we hear the rain before we feel it.

And thunder. Loud!

Jonah and I run toward the beach. Just like that, it's raining so hard I have to hold my hand like the bill of a baseball cap over my eyes so that I can see where I'm going. PJ is crouched under a tree, drenched. He's got his mask and snorkel on and a towel over his head. I kneel down next to him.

"PJ, it's okay. It's just rain. We've had lots of rain here, right?"

"But look over there," he says. "A tornado! Just like in *The Wizard of Oz*."

Out in the ocean, past Ginger Island and beyond Monkey Cay, is a furious black cloud. It's not hard to imagine the wicked witch and a few goats and pigs being tossed about in it. Everything around it is a blur. As I watch, Monkey Cay disappears in the rain, then Ginger. The sky is a huge gray wall moving our way.

"PJ," I say, "It's okay, really. It's not a tornado. They don't have tornadoes here. That's in the Midwest—Kansas, remember?" Man, I hope that's true. More thunder. The rain is really coming down, I can barely see Jonah a few yards away. He's untying the anchor line of the dinghy. I can't believe it. Where does he think he's going?

"Jonah! What are you doing?" The rain is so loud I have to shout even though he's very close. PJ has a death grip on my leg. I can barely stand up. "PJ, let go."

"No!"

"Fine, come with me, then." At least PJ can see with that stupid mask on. I can't keep my eyes open against the downpour. Who would believe it could rain this hard? The wind is blowing the rain sideways.

"Jonah," I say as I reach the dinghy, dragging PJ along behind me like a dead log. "Jonah, where are you going?

You're not going out there." The sea is dark—I can't see into it at all—and the wind has kicked up four-foot swells.

"We've gotta get to the boat. I've only got the one anchor out. It won't hold if this gets any worse."

"How are you going to put a second anchor out in *this*?" I say.

"I'll start the motor and use it to hold the boat into the wind until this squall passes. At least I'll be on the boat and can do something if the anchor cuts loose. Besides, we left all the hatches open. Bob's probably filling up with water right now." I look in the dinghy. There are already six inches of water in the bottom and it's still parked on the sand.

"PJ, get in the dinghy. Start bailing," I scream at him.

His eyes are as round as donuts. He gives me this crushed look as if I've slapped him, but he climbs into the dinghy and starts bailing water with the empty Clorox bottle that has its cap still on and the bottom cut off just past the handle so that it works like a scoop. I'm pretty sure he's crying but there's no way to tell with the rain pouring down his face.

The landscape around us is a dark gray blur. Out on the water, I can barely see Bob through the downpour.

"Casey, help me shove off."

I push from the bow of the dinghy. Nothing. With all that water and PJ in it, it weighs a ton. Jonah and I stand on either side of the boat and jostle it back and forth in the sand, inching it toward the water. A wave comes in and lifts the stern. Jonah and I shove hard, letting the incoming wave lift the boat and carry it out enough to float. PJ's still bailing. When he feels the boat launch, he looks up in a panic.

"I'll hold it, you jump in!" Jonah yells. I'm up to my waist in the water. I grab the edge of the dinghy and try to hoist myself in. It's hopeless. The little boat rises with the swells and I'm left hanging off the side until the swell passes and my feet can touch bottom again.

PJ's scared, but he's still scooping up water and tossing it overboard. "Don't let me go, Casey. Don't let me go," he says.

I know he's afraid he'll go out to sea and Jonah and I will be left onshore. So am I. Jonah is struggling to hold the boat; it's bobbing like crazy and the waves are slapping against the stern and sending up spray.

Suddenly I'm up to my neck in water—the boat is going out. *Don't let it go, don't let it go,* I chant to myself. I try flashing a smile at PJ as I push myself up the side of the boat, then fall back into the water. I imagine what PJ sees: my head popping up, then disappearing, my face in a wild grimace, my teeth clenched.

What I need is my fins; that's how I usually get into the dinghy, by giving a good hard kick and propelling myself upward.

I count to three mentally and give it all I've got. I pitch forward into the boat, roll and land on my back between the bench seats. My legs are sticking straight up in the air. It takes a minute to right myself. PJ can't help laughing. I forgive him silently, figuring it's good he's laughing.

Jonah crash-lands right next to me. It's a little gratifying to see that he didn't manage hoisting himself in any more gracefully than I did. He lands facedown at the same moment that PJ's bailing out a big scoop of water, one that includes Jonah's face. Jonah spits out water, and I give Jonah a hand up, trying not to let him see me swallow a laugh. Now that we're all in the boat togther I feel safe, until I look past Jonah and see that the sky is even angrier-looking than before.

Immediately Jonah yanks on the cord for the outboard and when it starts, we haul out of there fast. Bob looks like a dog straining on its leash. The mast is swaying back and forth and the anchor line is pulled taut at the bow.

The bow of our dinghy is tossed up and then plunged down into the troughs as we make our way slowly over the ocean swells toward Bob. When we've almost reached the anchor line, I look past Bob to Tartuga. I'm stunned to see that over Tartuga, the sky is a brilliant blue. It's perfectly clear, as if there is no storm. Ginger and Lizard islands are all but obliterated by the squall; I can't even make out the silhouettes of the trees. That awful black cloud is now passing directly over our heads.

The moment we grab Bob's stern, the rain stops. Just like that, as if some giant somewhere finally noticed he'd left a faucet running full blast and casually reached over and turned it off. But as short as that squall was, Bob is still a mess below deck. The cushions are soaked, the cabin floor is slippery and wet. The water in the head is three inches deep. PJ and I start mopping. I can hear Jonah in the cockpit pumping the bilges out.

Once the worst of it is cleaned up, PJ and I go topside

and help Jonah get organized. I take the helm and Jonah raises the sails. PJ is silent.

"PJ," I say. "That was kind of exciting, don't you think?"

"It was scary," he says. His lower lip is sticking out about a mile.

"Well, yeah, but in an exciting way, right? Like an adventure?"

"No."

Okay, new approach. "Well, at least nothing bad happened. The worst thing was that we left the hatches open and made a mess of the boat."

PJ is silent. Jonah and I exchange a look, the first eye contact we've made since he kissed me.

"Can we go see the turtles when we get back?" PJ says.

This little guy is definitely a strategist.

Mike greets us at the dock. His sand castle fort has been demolished. It looks like a mound of melted ice cream on the beach. He's all excited about the storm, though.

"Everything turned black. I couldn't even see the islands across the channel! The dock was bouncing up and down. We had to shut all the windows in the house and rain *still* got in!"

"I can imagine," I say. "The inside of the boat got pretty wet. Wanna help me drag the bunk cushions out into the sun?"

"Okay," he says. Not wildly enthusiastic, but willing.

We struggle with the sopping wet bunk cushions. Mike looks around at the cabin. I think PJ and I did a pretty good job of mopping up, but Mike says, "Uh-oh."

Dad's charts! They were sitting out on the navigation desk, right below an open hatch. I didn't even notice them before. They're plastered together. I can read each one through the one on top of it. Great. I'll have to peel them apart and lay them out in the sun too.

Half an hour later our little homestead looks like a refugee camp. The dock, the terrace, the railings, everything is covered with drying stuff. Sheryl has towels hanging off the outdoor furniture; all Bob's insides are spread out on the dock and the terrace; our laundry, which had been hung out to dry, is drenched—maybe with a little less salt water left in it, I hope. Dad and Jonah have gone over to Anderson's place to check things out. It probably looks the same way over there.

I clear a space on the patio table to lay out Dad's charts. We've got about two hours of daylight left. Maybe that'll be enough. Everything will have to come inside tonight. It rains almost every night.

Luckily the charts are printed on super-heavy paper, and they peel apart without tearing. They're soaked, though. Damn.

It's not until I lay the last one out—something about the way Dad's notations have smeared—that I realize: my letter from Matt! We left our stuff under a tree on Lizard. My letter's in my gear bag along with my mask and snorkel, though I'm certain I could live through the rest of the summer without those if I just had Matt's letter. I bite my bottom lip, feeling like PJ, trying to think of a way to get back to Lizard Island, when I remember the Whaler. It wasn't damaged at all. Jonah can run me over there; it'll only take a few minutes.

I race over to Jonah's just in time to see him and Dad take off, in the Whaler, heading for Tartuga. Rats!

PJ's waiting for me when I come back to the house.

"Can we go see the turtles?"

"Not now, PJ."

"But you said."

"No, I didn't say, you said. I didn't agree to it. I don't feel like going over there right now. Sorry," I say, and walk past him.

He calls out after me, *"But I can't go without you!"*

Don't I know just how he feels? Haven't I felt as if my whole life is in everyone else's hands? Mom decided where I'd spend my summer vacation. Dad decides I ought to take scuba lessons. Maybe I should; maybe I'd love to learn to scuba dive. But I wish *I* had thought of it—that it was something I wanted to do and *I* had asked Dad about it. I feel as if I never do anything on my own. Even when it's me and Jen, I rely on her to cook up our little schemes and adventures. She's always the one who does the talking to get us out of class. I'm the one who slinks out of class and follows her down the hall like a puppy.

I've even let Jonah decide things for me and he doesn't even know it. All week I wanted to go snorkeling at Mahoe but I didn't go; instead I waited for Jonah. Why didn't I just go on my own? Who am I, anyway? My mom, who lets Roger decide what she likes and lets Dad tell her what to do? Then, after I waited all week to go to Mahoe, where did I end up today instead? Lizard Island. An island I haven't even wanted to set foot on. And look what happened! Everything's soaked. We left all our gear on Lizard and I can't even go get it because I'm stranded on this island away from everything civilized.

And my letter!

If Jen were here, she wouldn't be moping around feeling sorry for herself; she'd be taking scuba lessons! I can't even decide if I *want* to take them. And look at Sheryl. She's helping Dad with his turtles, sure, but she's got her own thing going with her science journals and her articles. She goes off swimming on her own in the afternoons; she's doesn't wait around for Dad to take her anywhere.

I'm tired of being this way, of letting whatever happens, happen, instead of being the one to *make* things happen. What am I waiting for? It's *my* life. *I* should be the helmsman. Make that helms*woman*.

I find Sheryl in the kitchen, washing veggies. "Sheryl, I wonder if I could talk to you a minute."

"About Jonah?" she says, smiling into the sink, not looking up.

"About Bob."

"Your dad's boat?"

"Yeah," I say. "I was hoping I might get you to teach me how to sail him. For real, not just crewing. I'd like to be able to do all the parts." I think, What I really need to learn is how to be more like you and less like me, but I'll start with sailing.

"I want to know how to be able to get around on my own," I say. "The way you can."

When she looks up from the sink I can see she's pleased. "Glad to," she says. No hesitation, no wink. She just gives me a big smile and a head of lettuce.

"We'll start in the morning," she says. "Now, how'd you like to make the salad?"

12

When it comes to sailing lessons, Sheryl—nice, cute, sweet, wink-a-minute Sheryl—turns out to be a slave driver.

On the first day, we never leave the dock. Sheryl teaches me the name of every single part of the boat, right down to the little pins that hook the lifeline gate. They're called pelican hooks. Everything on a boat has a different name than it would have on land, like lines instead of ropes, galley instead of kitchen, head instead of bathroom. What would be a pulley on land is called a block. There are all kinds of little tricks for remembering things. Like "port is what you just left" and "red right returning" to remind you that the red entrance buoy should be on your starboard side when you come into port. The telltales, which are streamers on each side of the mainsail, *tell* you when you have the sail set properly and whether you need to trim it in or let it out a bit. "In in, out out" means if the outside telltales are waggling, instead of streaming smoothly, you need to let the sail out; if the inside ones are breaking, then you pull the sail in.

By lunchtime my head is crammed with sailing terms. I'm becoming bilingual! Memorizing these terms is nothing like trying to remember how to conjugate verbs in Spanish class, or what each of the Constitutional amendments are, or who all the Supreme Court justices are, the way we had to in Mr. Halverson's class. Not once did I look forward to that class the way I'm looking forward to getting on the boat again tomorrow. Now I feel as if I'm learning stuff that matters to me, that's going to affect what I do, and that I'm actually *doing* something—something completely different from anything I've ever done before, or even thought about doing.

I know that Sheryl gave up her morning for me and that means she has to work this afternoon. Jonah and Dad took the Whaler into town and won't be back until dinner. I still haven't been able to get my gear and Matt's letter. Anderson is nowhere to be seen, which is fine by me. So, after lunch and a quick turtle visit, I take PJ and Mike snorkeling at Mahoe. We see a green moray eel and a small stingray. They're thrilled.

The three of us snorkel and swim for the rest of the afternoon. Jonah has been coming for dinner a lot—I guess he doesn't find Anderson's company any more stimulating than I do. Jonah's really a good sport about joining our family game marathons afterward so I'm looking forward to that. In the meantime, since I have no witnesses, I suppose counting turtles, naming fish and playing in the water with my two little brothers aren't the worst things in the world.

By midweek, Sheryl has taught me to dock the boat by rocking the engine back and forth between forward and reverse, using the way the boat kicks to the side in reverse to line it up with the dock. After all that engine work, when we're ready to actually take Bob out on the water she insists that we can't use the motor.

"Assume it won't start," she says. "It's important to be able to do everything with the sails alone." Once we're away from the dock, she gives me a few instructions and plops herself down on the lazaret with a magazine. She's pretending to read, but she hasn't turned a page yet. I feel a little better knowing she's watching over the top of her magazine, but she won't lift a finger to do anything. Every now and then she says something really casual, like:

"You might want to think about tacking in a minute."

I've been so intent on keeping the sails filled and watching the masthead fly that I've failed to notice that we are on a collision course with an outcropping of rocks just off Cactus Cove. In a panic, I turn the boat without releasing any sails. Sheryl doesn't move, as if we're not about to sink Bob and be battered to death against the rocks.

Before the boat stops completely, I release the jib sheet. I have to let go of the tiller to trim the jib on the leeward side. Once again, I don't have the jib sheet wrapped around the winches and ready to go. The boat spins around and we're backwinded. Sheryl barely blinks, just glances around as if she's enjoying the scenery, which happens to be spinning past the boat at about a hundred miles an hour. Well, maybe at about five knots.

I release the newly trimmed sail again, let the boat right itself, tack and retrim. When I look to her for applause, she's concentrating hard on an ad for denture cream.

We cook along a bit and when I feel comfortable again I say, "Mind if I try tacking again, for practice?"

She looks up as if she's just now noticing that I'm on the boat and that I have her life in my hands. "You're the skipper," she says, shrugging, then winking (*finally*! I was beginning to worry that this wasn't the real Sheryl, that some alien had invaded her body).

I tack. No problem this time. I start the turn, let the jib sheet go with one hand, still holding the tiller with the other, and yank in the new working sheet while holding the tiller with my leg. Probably not the way the America's Cup helmsman does it, but he usually has about six linebackers tailing for him.

I tack a few more times, just so I feel comfortable doing it. I yell, "Ready about?" and answer myself, "Ready!" Hey, my Spanish teacher always says you won't really learn a new language until you start speaking it out loud. But today, unlike the day Jonah took us to Lizard Island, I don't say "ready" until I actually am. Then I say, "Helm's alee!" and start the process of bringing the bow of the boat through the wind and releasing first one jib sheet and then, after the jib has crossed the bow, pulling in the other sheet. By about the sixth time I do this, it's pretty smooth and I've figured out how to hold the tiller and work the sheets without doing an awkward balancing act that involves my leg, my foot and sometimes my butt.

After a while Sheryl says, "I think you've got coming about down pretty well, Casey. Why don't we break for the day so I can get some work done? We'll go out again in the morning."

"Sure," I say. "And, Sheryl, thank you so much again for doing this for me. I'm really having fun and every day I feel more comfortable on the boat."

"You're doing great," she says as we head back to the dock.

For the rest of the week we practice jibing. Sheryl does a few jibes first, with me standing right beside her at the tiller. On my first try, I'm so hesitant that I get caught with the wind directly behind me and nothing happens, the mainsail just starts flapping and we're dead in the water for a few dicey moments before a gust of wind catches it and sends it flying to the other side with a loud crack. Sheryl doesn't blink, she just says, "Why don't you try again?"

After I've done about thirty jibes without killing myself, or Sheryl, and the boat just happens to be pointing in the direction of Lizard Island, I ask Sheryl something I've been wanting to ask all week. "Umm, Sheryl, do you mind if we take the boat over to Lizard for a minute? We left all our snorkel gear over there during the storm."

"Sure," she says. "That'll give us a chance to go over anchoring procedures."

Naturally.

She lets me start the engine when we get close to the little beach where our stuff is. We drop the sails, find a good spot to anchor and turn the boat up into the wind. It takes me about three tries to get the hang of stopping the boat at the exact right spot. I have to line the boat up so that it's pointing straight into the wind, then make sure the bottom is sandy and there isn't a reef I could damage or some grass I might get the anchor tangled up in. Sheryl stands at the bow, ready with the anchor, and gives me a hand signal when it's a good spot. She drops the anchor in about twelve feet of water, the same way Jonah did. Then she starts letting out the anchor line and I back the boat down, revving the engine in reverse until we're sure the anchor has dug into the sand. We wait about five minutes to make sure the anchor is set. It'd be a big drag to go ashore and come back to find our boat's left without us.

As we do all this, I try to imagine doing it by myself. This part would be pretty hard, although using the engine I might be able to do it. *Might*.

When Jonah brought PJ and me over here, he never turned the motor on. He told me exactly what he was doing as we approached the anchorage, but he did all the work. Sheryl's twice as old as Jonah but for some reason I'm more impressed that she can do all this herself than I was that Jonah could. Which isn't to say that I wasn't impressed with Jonah. Maybe it's because Sheryl's a woman and he's a guy. That probably makes me a bit sexist. Jen would say, "Big-time."

Sometimes I think we have these limited ideas about things because we don't have any other examples to go by, only what we've seen. Mom, for instance. She'd never take sailing lessons. It wouldn't even occur to her; she'd just automatically think that a man, like Dad or Roger, would be the one in charge who would do the sailing. She'd be the passenger. I'm not sure she'd even *want* to be a passenger because, and I know this from personal experience, all the wind and salt water would be murder on her hairstyle. But she'd still come, if that was what Dad or Roger wanted her to do. She wouldn't ever think that she could be the sailor herself. To be fair to Mom, I have to admit that I would have thought the same thing if it hadn't been for Sheryl's example.

I don't want to be like that, though. I'm going to take Gina's philosophy about paying attention and about attitude and apply it to myself. I'm going to start noticing when I'm doing things just because someone else is ahead of me, leading the way, and decide if that's the way I want to go too. And if it's not, I'm going to choose a different route, and once in a while I'm just going to have to forge the path myself. Humph, I think. Then I realize—and it makes me smile—that this whole sailing thing was my idea and that I could get the hang of this.

Once we're sure the boat is secure we dinghy to shore. Our stuff is right there under the tree where PJ put it. I was worried it might have gotten washed away. I had planned to wait until we were back on Ginger before looking in the pouch of my gear bag, but that decision only holds up for about thirty seconds. As soon as we're in the dinghy heading back to the boat I look. There's my stuff: comb, small toothpaste tube, sunglasses case, towel, sunscreen and Matt's letter. Very damp.

I can tell it must have been soaked; the felt-tip ink on the outside is smeared. All that's left of my name is the big "C" and two digits of Dad's post office box on Tartuga. The waterproof pocket probably works great if you remember to zip it all the way closed.

Please don't let the inside be smeared, I chant to myself all the way back to Bob. *Please, please, please.*

We raise the main without starting the motor. Sheryl pulls up the anchor, and I fall off to port and head away from Lizard Island. It's only about a fifteen-minute sail back to Ginger, and Sheryl and I just ride quietly, without talking. She must sense that I've got things on my mind. But it's something else, too; I think we're feeling very comfortable with each other and . . . oh, I don't know, satisfied.

I only bang into the dock a little when we pull up. I've learned to aim the boat directly at the dock, then turn it at what seems like the last possible moment to get it right up against the dock. Luckily, I've got six of those brontosaurus tampons hanging over the side for insurance.

"Thanks again for giving me these lessons, Sheryl. I really appreciate your doing this for me."

"I'm enjoying it," she says. "You worked hard today. Jibing can be tricky. I think you're going to make a good sailor one day."

"Thank you," I say, feeling pretty good. I'm just realizing that except for anchoring, I actually took the boat out, tacked around and brought it back in one piece. Wait till I tell Jen.

"I'll make up the lines and square the boat away," I say.

"Great," she says. "I'll start lunch. I imagine PJ and Mike will be coming around any minute, starving."

I coil the lines and put them away, store the lazaret cushions below and make sure the hatches are closed, then sit topside to look at my letter.

I've been saving it, like a treat. My fingers have been crossed the whole time I've been working. I say one last silent *please* before I pull Dad's penknife out of the navigation desk and slit open the envelope. The knife doesn't make a sound when I slice the envelope because the paper is still damp.

I carefully slip the letter, which is two sheets (!), out of the envelope and gently unfold it, peeling one sheet away from the other as cautiously as if it were some ancient Biblical scroll.

Oh, Matt! He uses these felt-tip pens for everything! Only the top third of each page is not smeared into an indecipherable pale blue watercolor wash. I can feel tears pressing against my eyelids. No way am I going to cry, though, and wash away what's left of this letter.

The entire first paragraph is legible:

Hi, Casey,

Thanks for the postcards. Does it really look like that or are they touched up? If they're accurate, you must be in heaven. I can't wait to see your own pictures; I'm sure they'll be great. Are you taking any underwater pictures?

Most of the rest of the page is a blur. I can barely make out a few words: "checkers," "water balloon," "crybaby," "tetherball." I figure Matt's probably telling me about his job at the playground.

I don't find any capital "P"s for "Patty Harper." But then, who's to say he'd mention her? I didn't exactly give him a head-to-toe description of Jonah when I wrote to him. The top third of the second sheet is also legible:

and we couldn't stop laughing about it for the rest of the day.

I guess I should get back to work now. Anyway, I really meant what I said before.

Take care,

Matt

What! What did he say before? *What* did he really mean? I turn the paper over and over, holding it up to the sunlight.

I go back to the first page and look for clues. *Who was laughing so hard? At what?* The best I come up with is another part of a word from the first page: "ance." "France?" "Dance?" Maybe. Matt went to a dance? With *who*? Maybe not. Maybe they're teaching the kids on the playground how to *square dance.* Yeah. That's just the kind of corny thing they make kids do in those summer programs.

Maybe that's what they "couldn't stop laughing about." Maybe he and Patty Harper couldn't stop laughing over some cute kid on the playground. Some cute crybaby who plays checkers and tetherball and throws water balloons.

Probably some kid who threw a water balloon at Patty Harper's chest so that her T-shirt was soaked and she really got to show off her bra size.

Right. And maybe "ance" is the last part of "romance."

I think I'd better get off this boat; I'm starting to feel seasick.

13

The house is filled with people when I get back. While Sheryl and I were sailing, Jonah's mom arrived from Tartuga with Jonah's little brothers and sister.

For some reason the kids, including PJ and Mike, are wearing headbands with feathers in them. I'm surrounded by ten little Indians. I count heads. Well, six, including my own two brothers.

Jonah is standing in the middle of this little crowd. And it does seem like a crowd; I haven't seen this many people in one place since we left California. Jonah introduces me to everyone. His five-year-old twin brothers are Frankie and Johnny. The boy who's exactly PJ's age (as he announced proudly, holding up fingers) is Luke. Annie is eight and a half.

Looking at them all, circling me like I'm a covered wagon, I have an awful feeling. What if, instead of losing PJ as my constant companion and unknowing chaperone, I'm gaining this entire six-pack?

And then Jonah introduces me to his mom, Mary. She's perfect. She's fat, she has a wooden spoon in her hand and she's wearing an apron! I like her already. She looks totally capable of taking care of an entire tribe of Indians and a few cowboys, too. In fact, right in the middle of asking me how I'm enjoying my vacation, she beans Luke with her wooden spoon and tells him to pipe down or go outside. It's all I can do to keep from throwing my arms around her and saying, "Saved!"

"Everybody out until we call you in for lunch," she says, and all the little Indians "Woo, woo, woo" right out the door. Mike and PJ included. Bless her.

"I heard you've been getting sailing lessons?" Jonah says.

"Yeah," I say. "This morning we took the boat out in the channel and then over to Lizard. I picked up all the gear we left there. I've got yours in my room."

"Thanks. You know," Jonah says, "I would have been happy to teach you to sail."

"Oh, well, thank you," I say, trying to sound cool but grateful. "I think since I've already started, I'll stick with Sheryl." Anyway, I think, I'd be way too nervous around Jonah and I'm comfortable with Sheryl. It's easier to concentrate on what I'm supposed to be doing.

"So when are you going to take *me* out sailing?"

"Well, maybe after a few more lessons," I say. "How are the nets at Turtle Beach coming?"

"All done. When the turtle eggs hatch they'll have a safe, bird-free trip to the ocean. Then they're on their own, but at least they'll have a chance. If this works, and more hatchlings survive their first few hours, we might see a real change in the turtle population over time."

"That'll make PJ happy," I say.

"Yeah." Jonah smiles. "It's too bad we can't throw a big net over all the poachers out there."

"Jonah? Do me a favor, okay?" I say. "Don't mention the poachers to PJ. He's always worrying about what happens to the turtles naturally. I don't want him thinking about people hurting them so they can make combs and eyeglass frames and stuff."

"Sure, okay," Jonah says, but he says it in a funny way. Maybe he doesn't think I should be trying to protect my brother from the truth. "Hey," he says then, "I'm going into town this afternoon. Do you want to ride over with me? We can take your mail over." He smiles at me conspiratorially.

Mail! Yes, I need to write to Matt and tell him that I couldn't read his letter. And Jen. I should tell her things have picked up. I've been so busy sailing and swimming, and so distracted by Jonah, I've hardly written to her since I first got here. That seems so long ago—what did I say, anyway? I can't exactly check the "Sent" folder, like I can with e-mail. She probably thinks I'm miserable. I don't want her to think that. Of course, I'm not sure *what* I want her to think.

"Sure," I say. "I've been wanting to get over there."

"Great," he says, "meet me at the dock at two-thirty. We'll take the Whaler." He looks outside to where all the little Indians are now busy building a tepee out of sand and driftwood. "Just you and me," he says, quietly, almost in a whisper. Then he gives me a big smile.

"Okay," I say, my heart pounding. I turn away from him and walk into the kitchen so he won't see my face flush bright red, right through my perfect tan.

I spend every minute between lunch and two-thirty trying to decide what to wear to Tartuga. It's a good thing I'm not home with my whole closet to pick from; I'd never get out the door.

I finally decide on white shorts, my Teva sandals, a bright blue T-shirt and a neon pink baseball cap to keep the boat ride from making my hair look like I did it in the blender.

I toss a brush, sunglasses, lip gloss and my camera into a straw bag that Sheryl loans me. She gives me two library books to return. Dad gives me a stack of mail to post, and I stick that in the bag too, feeling guilty. I've had plenty of time, but I didn't write to anyone. I started to. I got the paper out. And a pen. Then I started trying on T-shirts.

When I get to the dock, Jonah is lying on his stomach with half his body hanging over the water. I snap his picture before he notices me. He's scraping barnacles off the hull of the boat with a weird-looking tool.

"That looks medieval," I say, staring at the sharp, curved blade.

"Yeah, pretty nasty, huh?" he says, swishing it in the water a couple of times and rolling over on his back. He sticks his hand out, and I help him up.

"We haven't had the Whaler out of the water for months; there's a whole ecosystem living on the bottom. It really creates drag on the boat. I was just trying to pry some of these barnacles off, but they're not going for it."

He climbs into the boat. I stow my stuff below the seat and jam my hat on my head, hoping he noticed how good my hair looked a second ago, since I'm going to have hat head by the time we get there.

"Ready?"

"Yup," I say, pulling my ponytail through the opening in the back of the cap and putting my feet up on the dash. "Ready."

Jonah stands at the wheel to drive the boat. His hair, I notice, doesn't mess up. That's because it's all one length and he has it tied in a short ponytail. Something Jen would hate but I'm finding very appealing.

It's too loud to talk on the way over, especially the way Jonah drives the boat—much faster than Dad.

Sailing is about the boat, the sea and trimming the sails just right to catch the wind. Riding in the Whaler is about speed and getting somewhere fast. I have to keep my hand clamped down on my cap to keep it from flying off my head.

Every now and then Jonah looks over at me and smiles. I smile back.

Out in the water, I think I see a turtle. I'm getting really good at spotting them. Just before they surface for air, there's what looks like a light spot in the water, as if there's a flat rock just under the surface. Then a head sticks out.

"Look!" I yell. In the split second when I take my hand off my head to point, my cap flies off and into the water. Jonah sees it and immediately spins the boat around. It's already just a little pink dot in the distance, we were going so fast.

"Man overboard!" he shouts, and slows the boat down as we approach my cap bobbing in the wake of the boat. He brings the boat up as close as he can and puts it into neutral. We drift slowly toward the cap.

"Do you think you can reach it?"

"Almost, in about four more feet," I say. I unsnap the hook we use to pick up moorings when we don't anchor and line myself up so that I can snag the cap as it floats by. When I'm leaning way out over the edge of the boat, Jonah kneels beside me on the seat and circles my waist with his arm, steadying me in the boat. I hook the cap and bring the pole into the boat.

Jonah is still holding on to me, and when I turn, his face is just inches from mine. We kiss. This time it's not just him kissing me. In fact, maybe it was even *me* that leaned into him just enough to get things started.

I think about Matt and how he's a little shy and how maybe if I started things instead of waiting for him, he wouldn't be so shy about kissing. But I can't hold that thought right now. All I can think about is that Jonah and I are out here drifting around in the middle of the ocean, and I can feel the hot sun against the back of my neck and Jonah's arm around my waist, against my skin, which is warm and dry, and I'm still holding the pole with my cap on the end like a pink flag, and he reaches past me with his free arm and shuts off the motor and all we hear now is a turtle sighing somewhere—or maybe that's me?—and we're still kissing.

A few minutes later we're still kissing.

A seagull lands on the outboard and we come up for air. Jonah lets go of me and shoos the bird away before it makes a mess on the boat. I shake my cap out over the side of the boat but it's already completely dry.

"Probably we should go on into town," he says.

"Probably," I say.

He starts the motor, and I smooth my bangs and put my cap back on. He sits next to me and we resume our trip, a lot more slowly than before, his hand resting lightly on the back of my neck all the way into South Harbor on Tartuga.

As we pull up to the public dock, Jonah cuts the engine. I hear a car horn honk twice. Two cars are inching their way around a goat standing in the middle of the road. A regular traffic jam.

I've gotten so used to how quiet it is on Ginger that even Tartuga seems noisy and congested, overpopulated. How would home seem to me now? I wonder. Deafening, probably.

We walk down to the same place Dad took us the first day we arrived. It seems like a hundred years ago. I was so tired that day, and depressed, and *white*! I look at my arms. All the hairs are bleached to a silvery blond. My skin is so dark against my shorts! I push my watchband aside and look at the pale skin underneath. The old me. But who is the new me? A girl who just this morning sailed from one island to another almost on her own, who just now stepped off a speedboat onto a third island with a boy who looks as if he could play the teenage Tarzan in a movie?

"Conch fritters?" Jonah says.

"Funny, that's what we had the day we arrived here from California."

"Does that seem like a long time ago?" Jonah says.

"Yeah, it really does. How did you know?"

"Last summer I stayed with friends who live near Albuquerque. I spent the whole summer working at their guest ranch. By the time I got home, I felt like a tourist. I even came back to the island wearing a pair of cowboy boots. Now I can't even imagine that I wore closed shoes for a whole summer, let alone boots. I remember thinking that it was really hot here."

"Well, it *is* hot here," I say. "But Albuquerque's hot too, isn't it?"

"Yeah, but dry. I finally got used to that dry heat and then I came home and couldn't stop sweating."

"How long does it take to get used to this heat?" I ask, casually wiping my sweat mustache with the back of my hand.

"It depends," Jonah says, giving me one of those looks he has, like he knows something that I don't, but that maybe I'm about to find out.

"Depends on what?"

"On how naturally hot *you* are."

A new sweat mustache pops up, fully formed, on my upper lip.

"So, what's a conch, anyway?" I ask, blotting my lip with a napkin. "Dad said we'd see plenty, but I haven't seen one yet. Have I?"

"We haven't seen any while we've been snorkeling together, but you've probably seen lots of them on your own.

In fact, doesn't Sheryl have one sitting on the windowsill in the kitchen?"

"That shell, you mean?" PJ's always got it smashed up against his ear because Dad told him he could hear the ocean in it. "*That's* a conch? What part are we eating?"

"The creature that lives in it."

I think of the crabs tucked into those little snail-like shells on Lizard Island. "Is it like a crab?"

"No. It's more like . . . well, I guess you'd say it's kind of like a clam, but not a clam, maybe a . . . I can't describe it, you're just going to have to wait and see one for yourself. It's really not like anything else you've ever seen before."

That's how I feel about everything I've seen on this whole trip: the island, the birds, the turtles and all those fish on the reefs. The way the sky is such a pretty, bright blue with its own landscape of fat clouds that change from moment to moment. And this amazing water everywhere! So clear and calm, like blue Jell-O. I'm never going to be able to make my friends understand by just describing it.

And then there's Jonah. He's so . . . so *comfortable* with himself. He knows all about the sea life around here; he can sail anywhere by himself and when he's working, he knows about everything: the generators, the pumps for the water, all the stuff he's doing for my dad at Turtle Beach. He's practically perfect. Not to mention great-looking.

Matt's face pops right back into my mind and tugs at me. I think he's perfect too, just in a different way. I look at Jonah. Matt's as cute as Jonah, I think. And Matt's got a lot of interests. He can draw really well, and he writes for the school paper. He's not as sure of himself as Jonah is, but he has a lot of good qualities, like being funny and considerate. Except for that popping into my brain thing. I could do without that at the moment. It's confusing enough liking two guys at the same time and not knowing whether I should just be enjoying the feeling or whether I should feel terrible about myself because it's so easy to be here, now, with Jonah when I know if I were home I'd be with Matt. I think about how Jen would love to be in this situation so I'm not complaining, just feeling a little mixed up.

After we eat, we walk around the town. Jonah seems to know everyone we pass and everyone who works in the stores. People going by in cars wave at him like they did at my dad.

There's a letter from Jen in Dad's P.O. box. I tear it open and read it while Jonah talks to someone in the dive shop.

Dear Casey,

Got your letter. You didn't sign it, but luckily I'm so brilliant I figured it was you. The flying fish stamp did it. Are there really flying fish there? Thanks for the weather report. Is that all you can talk about? It must be pretty boring there. There must be something to do. At least do some serious shopping and bring home some cute island sarongs or something. What about the beaches? Any cute boys?

We're having the usual summer here. I've only been to the beach twice, but Bobby (yep! we've been spending a lot of time together. :p) has a pool at his house and we've been going over there. He's got two

sisters that hang around oiling themselves up and talk-
ing on their cell phones all day so it hasn't been that ex-
citing hanging out over there, but at least we can swim.
I've got a great tan. How 'bout you?

Oh yeah, the picnic. No biggie. Bobby and I shared
a basket. Patty didn't come (don't ask me why, I don't
know). Matt was there but he played baseball the whole
time so we didn't talk except to say hi. He did ask me if
I'd heard from you but I hadn't yet. The next day I got
your card from the airplane, but I'd already mailed you
my card—did you get it? Huge bummer about the
cell service and not being able to get online, but don't
sweat it, you're not missing anything much around
here, believe me. Summer's practically over. I can't wait
to see you.

Love, Jen

She's right. It *is* almost over. Only three more weeks. Another big difference between today and the day I arrived. I remember looking around that first day and thinking that everybody's so-called paradise was the pits and that summer would never end. Now I think the real problem with paradise is having to leave it.

From the post office we cross the street to the library and drop Sheryl's books in the wicker basket on the front stoop. A skinny man in a straw hat who is sitting on the front steps says, "Jonah, you not tell me you have a next girl. Where dis pretty lady come from?"

"This is Casey," Jonah says, "Paul's daughter. I ran her

over so she could do some errands." I feel a little disappointed when he says I'm Paul's daughter instead of . . . instead of *what*? His girlfriend?

"I see," the man says. "Welcome, pretty lady. Jonah forget he manners." He sticks his hand out and says, "Cyril."

"How do you do, Cyril?" I say, shaking his hand.

"How do you find island living?"

"I like it very much. It's so beautiful here—it's paradise."

"Dat true," he says. Then to Jonah, "Be looking out, Tropical Storm Cindy, she coming dis way."

Jonah's head spins around as if he expects to see it coming right down the road. We say goodbye to Cyril and walk down to the public dock where we tied up the Whaler.

"Do you think we have to worry about Cindy?" I ask.

"Cindy? Huh? No, no," Jonah says. "Cyril was just talking."

"But this morning I heard on the radio that they've had to close the airport in St. Lucia."

Jonah just stares at me a minute. He is completely confused, as if he doesn't understand that I'm talking about a storm, which surprises me because it's something Jonah should know about.

"You don't know what I'm talking about, do you?"

"Do *you*?" he says.

"Yes. There's a storm coming. This morning, before Sheryl and I took Bob out, she listened to the weather station. They said Tropical Storm Cindy had reached St. Lucia and was moving north at about ten miles an hour. I forget how many inches of rain, but they said something about mudslides and stuff."

Jonah still looks a little blank, and then I'm sure that we're not talking about the same thing at all. He hasn't heard about the storm. He thinks Cyril was talking about a person.

"Who's Cindy?" I ask.

First he doesn't say anything. He looks uncomfortable, as if his skin doesn't fit right anymore and he'd like to shed it like a lizard.

Finally he says, "Cindy's my girlfriend. I thought Cyril was being facetious. I didn't know there really was a storm out there named Cindy. I thought he meant Cindy'd be mad if she saw me with you."

"Well, wouldn't she?" I say. My head feels like it's spinning now.

"She's off island. Her whole family goes north when school's out."

"That's not really what I asked."

"Well," Jonah says, taking my hand, "don't you think Matt wouldn't like seeing *you* with *me*?"

"I guess not," I say, feeling weird and stupid. I wish none of this had come up. I don't want to know anything about Cindy. And I don't want to think about Matt.

Except . . .

"Who told you about Matt?"

"The letter you wouldn't open," Jonah says. "The one you probably went back to Lizard Island for this morning."

"Matt's my boyfriend at home," I say.

"Yeah, I figured that out," Jonah says.

We're quiet as we square the boat away and leave the dock.

Jonah points out some frigates flying above us. They are pterodactyl-like, with their angular wings and long, pointed beaks.

I keep wanting to say something, but I'm not sure what. What did I expect? I can't be mad. Of course he has a whole life away from Ginger Island, just like I do. I shouldn't be surprised he has a girlfriend; I have a boyfriend, don't I? What did I think this was about for him? What is it about for me? We've both suspended our lives and stepped into this fantasy paradise bubble for a few weeks. Why did I think it was only me who had done that? I look over at him. He's still scanning the sky and sea, looking for things to show me. He's made this whole time here a lot more enjoyable for me—a lot. He sees me watching and gives me a little smile. I can tell that he does like me. I like him. I smile back.

Halfway home, in the middle of the channel, Jonah slows the boat way down and faces me in the seat.

"Casey, this is what I think: I really like you. In a few weeks you'll be gone, I'll be moving off Ginger and back to my family's house on Tartuga, school will start, Cindy will come home, and my life, *and yours*, will go back to the way they were before this summer began. I would like us to have a good time until then." He takes my chin and tips my head up to look at him. I've been looking at my feet, I realize.

"How about we don't worry too much about Matt or Cindy? They're probably having their own good times this summer. . . . I won't ask you about him and you won't ask me about her. Deal?"

I notice I have tan lines where my sandal straps are.

I think about Jen hanging out with Bobby—that means

Patty Harper isn't. I wonder if that was what Matt was talking about when he said *I really meant what I said,* that we should each be having our own "good time." Our own summer (rom)ance.

Jonah tips my head up again. "Deal?"

I feel as if I don't have time to think about this, really . . . and it's so much easier not to.

"Deal," I say, and stick my hand out to shake.

He looks at my outstretched hand and laughs, then uses it to pull me toward him so he can kiss me. The boat is still moving along, all on its own, back to Ginger Island.

14

For two weeks, Sheryl and I sail in the mornings while Jonah, my dad and Anderson work around the island. In the afternoons, Jonah and I swim or look at the turtles or hike and explore the island with all four of the little kids. There isn't a pebble or a dirt clod left on this island that doesn't have a name.

Jonah never seems to mind when we have got the whole troop with us, but whenever we can, we slip off by ourselves and walk along the beach or take a swim.

In the late afternoons the light changes and the whole world becomes a monochromatic silvery blue-gray. The water is at its stillest then, and Jonah and I will wade out into the warm silky water up to our necks and talk and laugh while we watch for the green flash. I haven't seen it yet, but maybe that's because every time that big orange sun slides past the horizon, I've got my arms twined around Jonah and my eyes closed.

At the end of these last two weeks of sailing, Sheryl drags a patio chair out to the dock one morning and makes herself comfortable.

"You're on your own today," she says, coating herself with sunscreen and positioning her big straw hat. "Take it out, sail east until your beam is lined up with Cistern Point, jibe, head back this way as far as Ring Dove Rock, tack, you decide when, then bring her—I mean him—back in."

I notice she's brought binoculars, a whistle and the handheld VHF with her. "Bon voyage," she says.

The only really stupid thing I do is forget to untie the stern line before I leave the dock. It takes me a minute to figure out why I'm not moving, even though I have a strong breeze. At least I didn't shove off without the motor running, which I'm now allowed to use since I've learned to get going under sail alone.

I don't think about the fact that I'm on the boat by myself. I do everything the way I've been doing it with Sheryl on board. It's so much easier, though, by myself, because I'm not thinking about whether I'm doing things right; I'm just doing them. Everything I've learned is falling into place.

I head downwind and when I'm abeam of Cistern Point, I jibe the boat and head back. I can't help looking toward the dock to see if Sheryl's watching, but she's too far away and I can't tell. I beat upwind toward Ring Dove Rock at a good clip, passing the dock and waving as I go by. PJ and Mike are out on the dock now. I wish Jonah could see me.

I have this overwhelming urge to just keep on going, past Monkey Cay, past Carvelle Rock, right on down the channel to the next string of islands. This feels so good. I'm sailing! On my own! I'm beating along with the wind just off the bow and my sails in tight. I watch the telltales on the mainsail and keep them streaming on both sides of the sail. If one side or the other breaks, I move the tiller just enough to get them streaming again without even thinking about whether I need to come up or fall off to do it. I just know without even reciting any rhymes. My face actually hurts, I'm smiling so hard.

Mike, PJ and Sheryl are clapping and cheering when I pull in. Dad's there too. He takes the dock lines for me and gives me a big hug. They're making a huge fuss over me, and I'm not even embarrassed. I'm so jazzed. I want to go right back out and do it again.

"Sheryl, thanks so much," I say, hugging her hard enough to knock her hat off. "You're such a good teacher." And really, she's been a good friend, too. I want to tell her that, and that I'm really glad she married my dad, but I'm not sure how all that would sound—it makes me feel a little disloyal to Mom, so I decide to keep the mush meter from going nuts and just say, "I know this has taken up a lot of your time and I really, really appreciate it. And you really are a good teacher. You're so calm and patient, it gave me a lot of confidence to just learn what I needed to without worrying that you were about to get mad or get nervous about something."

"I remember when I was learning to drive a car," she says. "My father could not stop telling me when to slow down, signal, look in the mirror, start braking—I never felt that I could really do it until after I had my license and he finally let me take his car around the block by myself. It was the first time I'd driven without worrying about getting yelled at and without having to think about every little move I made, instead of just letting it flow smoothly."

"When he taught you to sail, was he the same way?"

"Actually, it was my older sister who taught me to sail," she says, giving me one of her famous winks. "She didn't let me go out alone, but she went down below and wouldn't come up until we were back in the marina. I still remember how that felt. I felt like I could do anything."

Which is exactly how I feel this minute.

I'm surprised to look down and see that I'm standing on the dock because I feel like I'm walking on air.

"Let's eat," Sheryl says. "I've got conch salad and key lime pie for dessert."

"My favorite," Mike says. We hike back to the house, me leading the way, my deck shoes floating three feet above the ground.

"Congratulations, Cap'n," Jonah says when he comes around in the evening. "I hear you went solo today."

"Yup," I say, still grinning.

"Sorry I couldn't be here to see your maiden voyage. Anderson had me working all day on the water pump at the house."

"It's okay," I say, thinking of the fuss everyone made. I would probably have felt self-conscious about it with Jonah there. Brothers are one thing, boys are another.

"Well, I would have liked to be there. I also had to run

my mom and the twins back to Tartuga. She left Luke and Annie here. They'll be staying with us another week, which will be nice for PJ and Mike."

"Really, it's okay," I say.

"There's a full moon tonight. Want to take me out for a little spin?" Jonah says, taking my hand.

"Sure," I say. "If Dad'll let me. I only sailed back and forth in front of the beach, it's not like I took Bob to Tartuga or anything."

Jonah gives me a funny look. "I think you're forgetting something."

"What?"

"*I* can sail the boat, remember?"

"Oh yeah," I say. "Sorry."

"Just giving you a hard time. The truth is I'm very impressed." He looks around to see if anyone's looking before giving me a quick kiss. "You should feel really proud of yourself," he says.

I do, I do, I think, but I just smile at him and squeeze his hand.

We invite the boys and Annie to go with us. I have my fingers crossed that they'll say no and they do. The four of them are going over to Mahoe to look for crabs. Bless Mary for leaving Annie and Luke.

These past couple of weeks with the other kids here have been heaven. PJ and Mike are having a great time and they aren't bugging me every minute. I've finished two more books. Now I'm in the middle of *Jack* by A. M. Homes. I even wrote to Mom and told her things were great. I filled my letter with a lot of technical sailing talk. Maybe I'll inspire Mom to take up a sport of her own choice. She can teach it to Roger if she wants him along for company!

I wrote long letters to Jen, Gina and Matt, and told them about the island, the turtles, the stuff I've seen snorkeling, sailing and the storm we got caught in. Jen might think my weather reports are boring, but around here, weather *matters*.

I didn't mention Jonah, even to Jen. When I get home I will. Maybe. Part of me is dying to tell her about him, the way I tell her everything, but another part of me wants to keep him secret and separate from my other, real life.

This whole summer has been so unreal, anyway. I mean, the island, the weather, the sea creatures, the way we spend our days—it's unreal and more real at the same time. More real because the colors of the sea and the sky and the plants are so intense. And Jonah just feels like he's part of this place and I want to keep him here, in this private, secret paradise. I think that's why I can like Jonah so much without changing the way I feel about Matt. All my feelings for Matt are at home in my other, *actual* life.

Well, that's what I've been telling myself, anyway. But then Matt will just pop into my mind at the weirdest times. Like when I'm with Jonah. I feel bad because Matt and I have only kissed seven times and I don't even know how many times I've kissed Jonah. But way more than seven. How would I feel about Matt kissing Patty Harper ten times— or all summer long?

PJ looks at me apologetically as he traipses off behind Mike, banging a bucket against his leg and looking back every few steps. He is, after all, dumping me for Luke and Annie. I hope he can't tell that I don't mind one bit. I'm glad he's having a good time and has someone his own age to play—*hang*—with.

"Sorry, kids," Dad says when we ask him about taking the boat. "Normally I'd say sure, but there's some heavy weather coming our way, and I'd hate for it to surprise you out there. Better to stay on land tonight, just in case."

"No problem," Jonah says to me when we're outside. "We'll take a moonlight swim. I know just the place."

We hike across the island to the little beach the boys christened After Beach. Jonah says it's called Spring Bay. We've hardly been here at all since the day we discovered it. The bottom is all sand, no reefs or rocks, so the snorkeling is bad. When we come through the trees and out onto the beach, I can barely believe my eyes. The sand is luminous in the moonlight. We don't even need our flashlights to find a comfortable spot to sit. We lay the towel on a smooth rock and sit with our feet dangling over the edge.

We can't sit on the sand, even on a towel, because of the no-see-ums. They're these minuscule bugs that come out after sunset and bite you unmercifully until you throw up your arms in surrender and flee the beach. Nothing works against them. Insect repellant is an aphrodisiac to them.

Jonah puts his arm around me. We don't talk, just look out to the sea and listen to the quiet night sounds: the water lapping against the beach; the birds settling in; the land crabs, and the lizards, shifting leaves and twigs around in their travels. Every now and then we hear a *kerplunk*-type splash out in the water. It's remora feeding on fry and other small fish. We never see them during the day. Sometimes at night we shine the flashlight into the water around the dock, and they swarm to it, hoping for our leftovers from dinner.

The first time we saw them, Mike, PJ and I thought they were baby sharks. Now we know. They have a strange, ugly sucker panel on top of their bodies that they use to attach themselves to sharks and rays. Of course, we figured, if there are so many remora, there must be sharks for them to attach to. Dad said no, that he's never seen a single shark here. Still, when you see so many remora around, you can't help wondering.

Jonah says, "Want to take a dip?"

I look at the water, dark silver in the moonlight. The moon casts its own white streak for as far as we can see. It looks like a magical path that we could use to walk across the water until we reached the moon. I wish we could. Step right out onto that bright swath of moonlight and see where it took us.

"Dip?" Jonah says again.

"Oh, sorry!" I say. "It's so beautiful out, I must've been daydreaming." Then I remember the remora. And the sharks.

"Have you ever seen any sharks around?" I ask.

"Is that what you're worried about? I thought you might be thinking I'd said we should go for a *skinny dip*. Not that I wouldn't want to," he says, looking at me in a way that makes me swallow. Then he says, "Don't worry about sharks, Casey. I've never seen one. Besides, there's always a warning before they come around."

"There is? Really?"

"Yeah, that music, you know, *Nuh nuh, Nun nun nun nun nuh nuh*," he chants, imitating the theme from *Jaws*.

"Very funny," I say, but I *am* laughing and he kisses me. We lean back until we're lying on the rock and our feet are draped over the side, my toes just skimming the surface of the warm shallow water around the rock.

When he slips his hand under my T-shirt, I think about everything my friends and I have talked about. How you're supposed to clamp your elbow to your side and make a barricade between his hand and your bra so he can't go any farther; how then he'll look at you with all this adoration, because you're such a nice girl, not easy like some other girls he's probably gotten to second, maybe even third, base with. Then, after he's tried to do this on about ten different nights, you can finally let him, if you want to, and he'll still respect you.

But I'm not wearing a bra—I'm wearing my one-piece bathing suit, and Jonah and I don't have a whole semester of Friday-night dates lined up in front of us like yard lines on a football field, and I think he already does respect me because I've learned to sail and I didn't panic in the squall and I walked all the way over here in the dark when I know how many lizards are on this island.

I leave my arms right where they are, around his neck. He slowly brings his hand up higher. I know he can feel my heart beating in his palm. I can feel his in his neck.

For a moment I'm not aware of anything around us, not the rock under my head or the sea or the breeze that's picked up. Only Jonah, kissing me hard, and the feeling that I really could walk right out there across the water straight to the moon. Then, suddenly, there's Matt, right where Jonah should be! Not the real Matt, of course, but the Matt in my mind, the Matt whose dark lashes rest on his cheeks, who said he'd miss me, who gave me these damn earrings. And then I know.

Whatever I've been telling myself about Matt and what he might be doing this summer, and about me and Jonah and what we're doing, I realize that the truth is there's no way *I* wouldn't mind if Matt was sticking *his* hand under Patty Harper's shirt. And the same must go for him.

I sit up, bringing Jonah with me. He looks at me for a long minute, then nods as if he's heard every thought in my head, maybe even seen Matt's face. I smile at him, then take his hand and pull him to his feet.

"Let's swim," I say, pulling my T-shirt off over my head. He does the same, and we slip into the velvety sea. The water is as warm tonight as it was during the day.

We don't even notice the rain coming down until we're back on the beach gathering up our stuff. We run, laughing, stopping off at Mahoe to make sure the boys and Annie have packed it in. They have. By the time we get to the house, it's really coming down hard, but it's warm and we're drenched anyway so it doesn't matter.

We take our time walking back, not talking. When we get to the dock, Jonah starts to lean in to kiss me, then stops and looks at my face.

"I sense a sea change," he says.

"Yeah, I guess you do."

"Is it because I . . ."

"No, no, that's not it. Really. It's because of—"

"Matt," he finishes for me.

"Yes." I kind of shrug and give him a smile that I hope makes me look both apologetic and regretful at the same time. He nods and takes my hand in both of his.

"You know, Casey, a lot of times during the past few weeks I've wished that you weren't going back to California, that you lived here on the island and come September we'd be starting school together, that we'd be together. I think that might've happened if you weren't going home."

"I know. Me too. I like you so much," I say, looking down at my hand in his. "It's been a perfect summer. But I am going back, and soon, and I'm starting to think about home again as a real place. It's seemed so far away until tonight. I think I've been pretending that I was two people, the me who lives there and the me who's been having such a nice time here but who isn't really here. Tonight those two me's kind of crashed together. Do you understand that?" I ask, looking up and straight into his eyes.

"Yeah, unfortunately, I do," he says, looking right back at me and holding my gaze. "And I know you're right. You're just a little stronger than I am." He gives me a really sweet smile. "You're really something, you know that, Casey," he says, and brings my hand up to his chest and presses it there for a second. "And it has been a perfect summer. I have a feeling I'll be thinking about you long after you've gone home." He kisses my hand, then turns and walks away down the path.

I'm looking forward to climbing into bed and just being alone with my thoughts about this whole day—and night. I tiptoe to the door, figuring everyone's already tucked in for the night, either sleeping or reading.

Every light in the house is on, though, and Dad's listening to the radio. Sheryl's zipping his laptop computer into a waterproof bag. There are two more bags packed, sitting by the front door.

"What's going on?" I say.

"Tropical Storm Cindy has strengthened, possibly into a hurricane," Sheryl says. "Your dad and I have to go to St. George, where they're holding some turtles, and tag them. They don't have the equipment we have. They're afraid their pens won't hold up through the storm and the turtles will be hurt so they want to let them go. If we can get them tagged first, we'll still be able to track them and not lose all the data we've already collected."

"Is the storm going to hit St. George?"

"No, they're expecting it to pass a good hundred miles south of there, but the weather will be severe. We'll feel it here on Ginger, too. You're going to have to take care of battening down for me. Can you do it?"

"Yes," I say. How many times have I read the storm preparation list that's taped to the basement door? About three thousand, probably, the same way I read the stuff on the cereal box in the morning, *every morning*, or the titles on the back of a CD case when I'm just sitting there, listening to music.

I stand in front of the list now and start reading.

"Your dad's already taken care of the first couple of things," Sheryl says. That would be turning off the LPG gas valves for the stove and closing off the openings to the cisterns. Good thing. I might have read it three thousand times but I don't know how to do either one of those things.

"Probably the most important thing," Dad says when he turns off the radio, "is to monitor the weather channel and make sure you've got flashlights handy. I've already made sure there are plenty of water bottles downstairs."

I excuse myself so I can go change into dry clothes. Even though it's still raining outside, I hang my swimsuit and my T-shirt on the little drying rack we each have outside our room.

I towel my hair off, change into a long T-shirt and go back out to talk to Sheryl and Dad. Mike and PJ are in the living room now, looking a little anxious.

"So, Dad," I say, trying to sound as if nothing unusual is going on, "are you taking Bob tonight, or what?"

"No. Anderson is sending Jonah over to run us across the channel in the Whaler. We won't make the last ferry, and there are no flights going out tonight so we've arranged for a trawler to take us from Tartuga to St. George. It'll be after midnight when we arrive. I won't call then, but I'll radio you at eight tomorrow on channel twenty-two."

"Okay," I say. What *can* I say?

"If you run into any problems, if you feel scared, whatever, all three of you go straight over to Anderson's, understand?"

"Yes."

"If it's raining and you don't want to go over there, hail him on the radio. He'll be monitoring channel sixteen. You're square on the radio, right?"

"Yes, Dad." I'm so unused to my dad sounding this focused and serious that I'm actually starting to feel a little scared. He's just being extra-careful because he's having to leave us, I tell myself. That's probably why Jonah's taking them over instead of Anderson. That way there's still one adult here. Not my favorite adult, but at least he knows what to do.

"Okay, kids," Dad says when Jonah arrives and starts gathering up their bags and equipment. "I'm counting on you guys to behave and cooperate with Casey. And, Casey, we're really not expecting any problems, but if the weather does get bad you know what to do, right?"

"Roger," I say, giving them both a kiss goodbye, wishing I could talk to Jonah for a minute. We just smile at each other.

Mike, PJ and I stand in the doorway and watch the three of them in their yellow foul-weather gear disappear into the wet, black night.

I wonder where that fat, white moon went?

15

Mike, Mr. Future Boy Scout, is really getting into emergency mode. He's found all Dad's flashlights (about twenty of them—I guess Dad was a Boy Scout too), and he's testing the batteries. He puts a flashlight next to each of our beds, four by the door to the basement, one in every room on the floor by the doorway. The rest he scatters around so that now, if we're suddenly plunged into darkness, we're sure to kill ourselves tripping over flashlights.

At midnight, the rain stops.

Except for a few slats, we've got all the shutters closed and it's gotten really hot and muggy inside the house, even with the ceiling fans. Mike and PJ run around opening shutters. Outside, it's a bright moonlit night, just like before.

"Okay," I say. "Storm's over. Time for you guys to get into bed." I get dirty looks but PJ trundles off and, after a bathroom stop, a glass of water and a last-minute spot-check of the flashlight battalion, Mike goes too.

Alone at last.

I sit next to the radio for a while and listen to the traffic on Channel 16, the emergency channel. Just the usual stuff: boats hailing each other and switching stations to talk, someone reporting a big log floating in South Harbor, nothing interesting. Then I hear "Casey Stern, Casey Stern, this is Jonah. Come in, please."

"Jonah! I mean, this is Casey, over."

"Casey, switch to Channel seventy-eight, over."

"Roger," I say. "Over." I punch the preset button for 78.

"Casey, are you there?"

"Yeah, hi. Anything wrong?"

"No, I just got back, though. Just wanted to talk to you. Everything okay over there?"

"We're fine," I say. He's only about a hundred yards away, through the trees. I can't resist reaching out and touching the radio.

"Call me on sixteen if you need anything; I can be there in two minutes."

"Thanks," I say. "Night."

"Night, Casey. Sweet dreams. Over and out."

"Over," I say, even though I know he's clicked off already.

After he signs off I sit there a minute holding the mike in my hand.

Before going to bed with all the shutters open, I step outside to make sure there's no weather coming. The sky is clear. Big puffy clouds are lit up by the moon, like snowy mountains in the sky. It's humid and very, very still.

"Sweet dreams," I say into the warm air and to Jonah, out there down the path and through the trees.

Dad calls at 8:02 a.m. Mike and I are waiting at the radio.

"How's everything?"

"Fine," we both say.

"We've got a full day's work to do here. Will you kids be okay for one more night?"

"We're fine, Dad," I say. "It's not even raining. It stopped after you left."

"I'm surprised. We're really getting hammered here," he says. "But I heard they expect it to pass by this afternoon. We're hoping to wrap up by this evening and head out in the morning. You're sure you're okay?"

"We're *fine*, really."

"Casey?" It's Sheryl. She gives me a long list of food we have on hand and things I can make even though Dad turned off the gas valve for the stove.

"No problem, Sheryl, *really*," I say.

"Okay, good. Here's your dad."

"Casey, I'll call again at eight tonight," Dad says.

"Okay, Dad. We'll be here," I say.

I guess it's reasonable they're so worried since we are practically alone on the island. We're used to being left alone, though. Mom does it all the time when she has to work overtime or has a date. My brothers would rather eat sandwiches than cooked food any day of the week so they're not going to care that we have no stove. I sure don't care; it means I won't have to cook, just slap together some peanut butter and jelly sandwiches.

* * *

We spend the morning goofing around. Killing time is more like it. I'm hoping Jonah will come around so he and I can go swimming, although with Dad and Sheryl gone, I feel like I have to stay even closer to Mike and PJ. Luke and Annie usually don't come around until after lunch.

Mike's been working on a Huck Finn–style raft for the last few days and he talks PJ and me into taking it on its maiden voyage. He's tied boards together with rope and covered the whole thing with an old piece of sail canvas that Dad gave him. It looks okay, like it might actually float.

PJ and I sit square in the middle. Mike gives us a good shove away from the beach, and we drift out about ten feet before the boards in the middle separate and we drop into the water, the sailcloth folding up around us like a laundry bag.

It's hard to tell if PJ's coughing because he took in water or because he's laughing. I'm trying not to laugh myself because Mike looks so unhappy. It's not like he built the *Titanic* or anything. Well, maybe it is, judging by the way he looks.

We drag the wreckage to shore.

"It floated real good until it sank," PJ says.

"Gee, thanks," Mike says.

"How about," I say, stretching out the words, trying to sound like I've got a great plan, "we eat the rest of the key lime pie?"

"Now?"

"Yeah, why not? We're on our own. We'll have dessert and then if we feel like it, we'll have lunch. And if we don't feel like it, we won't. Okay?"

Mike kind of rolls his eyes at me. He can't stand it if he

thinks I'm trying to sound like a grown-up. I did kind of sound like Mom when she's trying to persuade PJ to do something. I know Mike will be happy to eat key lime pie just the same so I make a face at him and he makes one back at me.

"And can we see the turtles, too?"

"Sure PJ, whatever you want." I look at my watch: 10:15. It's going to be a really long day.

By the time we get over to the turtles, I can tell we're in for more rain. It hasn't started yet, but the sky to the south has darkened, and it's super-humid and hot. The seas are kicking up too, with the wind. There are small waves breaking on Cactus and After beaches. It's always windier on this side of the island because it faces east, the direction the wind comes from.

"There's turtles missing," PJ says as soon as we sit on the platform.

"You probably just can't see them," I say, not really looking. From here we can see Anderson's house and when I look that way, I can't help hoping I'll see Jonah. I'm so used to keeping my eye out for him—it's what I've been doing since he arrived on Ginger. I thought he'd be working with his uncle this morning.

"No, Casey," PJ says firmly. "There's two turtles gone. I know there were seven yesterday."

"Okay, PJ, I believe you. Anderson and Dad probably let them out. Maybe they were ready to go."

"I don't think so," he says.

"We can ask Dad tonight, when he calls," I say.

"Can *I* talk on the radio to him?" PJ says, giving me one of those looks.

When he says that about the radio, I remember that I didn't listen to the weather station this morning. Plus, we left all the shutters open; if it starts raining we'll be cooped up all afternoon mopping up the wet floors.

"I've got to go back to the house for a few minutes. Will you guys stay here till I get back?"

"Yes."

"*Can* I talk on the radio?"

"Yes, PJ, you can talk on the radio, tonight. I'll be right back, you and Mike stay here till I get back."

I jog back through the trees, skipping the scenic route but looking back a couple of times, still hoping I'll catch sight of Jonah. Nope.

Even though I've made up my mind about him, I haven't stopped having feelings for him and there's a little part of me . . . no, actually a big part of me, that wants to take back my decision, rewind to last night and just put my arms around him again. But no, even if my heart hasn't quite caught up with my head, I know this is the right thing and I need to start downshifting for when I go home. I'll say this, though: Matt and I are going to do a lot more kissing when I get back.

Channel Two's weather is recorded and already four hours old. Weather moves in so quickly, anything could have changed. I flip around looking for the up-to-date weather station. Finally I find it.

"Tropical Storm Cindy bore down on St. George with heavy rains and gusty winds this morning, causing mudslides and flash floods in rural areas with up to fourteen inches of rain. The storm is moving west-northwest at sixteen miles per hour and is expected to reach the Leeward Islands late tonight. Wind gusts of up to sixty-five miles per hour have been reported, and heavy rain is expected throughout today in the northern island chain." I click off the radio.

Great, it's going to be another wet, steamy night, trapped indoors. I close all the shutters and bring in the clothes that are hanging outside.

And then I hear it, a high-pitched whistle. It takes me a second to realize what it is. It's such an unusual sound on the island because it's so distinctly man-made. Then three short blasts—more like shrieks. I touch the whistle hanging around my neck, the one Dad gave us the day we arrived and that I've never much thought about except when I'm swimming and I tuck it into my suit so that its shininess won't attract a barracuda.

I run back down the path. Three more blasts. I'm trying to imagine what it could be. We're only supposed to use them in an emergency. I don't really believe anything's wrong. PJ's probably spotted the missing turtles or he and Mike are screwing around. I can feel myself getting mad, ready to yell at them. Even so, I blow hard into my own whistle to let them know I heard them and run as fast as I can until I reach White Bay.

PJ's lying faceup on the sand. He's not crying, but he's got his lower lip sucked so far into his mouth it looks like he swallowed his chin.

"What happened?"

"I think he broke his arm," Mike says. Mike sounds like he might be ready to cry himself.

"What do you mean, 'broke his arm'?" I kneel down next to PJ and look at him. He has pie tins for eyes. His arm is draped across his stomach. How can I tell if it is broken?

"He fell," Mike says. "He landed on his arm. It didn't sound very good."

"PJ, can you wiggle your fingers?" I ask, touching the back of his hand lightly. His wrist is swelling up, I can see that much.

"I don't think so," he says. "It hurts." His voice sounds so quivery I want to scoop him up, but what if his arm really *is* broken and I hurt him?

"I'm sorry, Casey," he says, "I just wanted to get a better view of the turtle pen so I climbed up in that tree and it broke."

He means a branch broke, I see when I look past him and spot it lying on the beach. Fresh wood shows at the break, like a giant splinter.

"Mike, stay here with PJ. Don't let him move. I'm going to get Anderson." I dash up the embankment over to Anderson's and pound on the door.

Luke opens the door while I'm still pounding, like he was standing right behind it. "Luke, get your uncle. PJ fell and we need a ride over to the clinic."

Luke just stares at me.

"*Hurry up!*" I shout at him, already pushing past him into the house.

"He's not here. He went with Jonah."

"Which beach?" I ask, turning to run back out, reaching for my whistle.

"There." Luke points out to the ocean.

"What do you mean? They're not on the island?"

"No, they left in the Whaler."

Damn. Damn, damn, damn. What am I going to do now? I can't imagine they would have left Luke and Annie alone if they were going to be gone long. The radio! I'll hail them, they'll come back. They can't be very far; they must have just run off for a few minutes. I run back down to the beach, looking out at the sea in every direction. No sign of them, just the weather, building to the east. There are black clouds in the distance, maybe five miles away.

"Mike, we need to get PJ back to the house. Help me get him up." We do our best to right PJ and then Mike takes PJ by the shoulders and guides him along the path. I can see he's being really careful, so I run ahead to get to the radio. They'll have the handheld VHF radio with them in the Whaler. I just hope they're not far.

Because all the shutters are closed, I can't see too well when I burst through the door, and I kick something hard with my bare foot.

"Ouch! Damn." I flip on the light and see what it is. The handheld VHF! It's *here*. That's right! Sheryl had it yesterday when I was out on the boat. Mike must have put it right by the front door.

Okay. Okay. Maybe Jonah and Anderson are coming back soon. I go outside with Dad's binoculars and scan the ocean in every direction. Nothing.

Mike and PJ arrive, creeping up the walk and into the

house. Mike sits PJ down on the couch and rushes off into Dad's office. He comes back with the first-aid kit and starts spreading stuff around on the floor.

Mike brings me a bottle of pills. "These are painkillers, Casey. Dad showed them to me. I think we should give them to PJ."

I read the label. "PJ, how much do you weigh?"

"Fifty-two pounds."

"Okay, Mike, get some water and give PJ *one* of these. We'll give him another in four hours. You be in charge of the time." Of course, I think, in four hours we'll all be sitting around at the clinic writing stupid stuff on PJ's cast and a nurse can give PJ all the pain pills in the world, but I can see Mike likes having the responsibility. He sets his watch alarm.

Mike disappears into the basement for a minute and comes back with a board and some sailcloth. PJ and I are silent as Mike cuts the cloth into strips with his Swiss Army knife. I'm thinking scissors would be a lot easier, but I don't say anything. He uses Dad's duct tape to tape the ends of the wood slats so that the jagged edges are covered. Then he carefully lays PJ's forearm on one board and tops it with the other, like a sandwich. Very slowly he wraps the cloth strips around and around, taping them when he's done.

"Splint," he says to his silent audience. "Boy Scouts."

Out of one of Dad's long-sleeved T-shirts, Mike makes a sling, tying the arms around PJ's neck.

I want to hug him. But I don't.

"Okay, you guys," I say, making up the plan even as I'm telling it to them. "This is what we're going to do. Mike, get some shoes on you and PJ, then grab some blankets. We're going to motor Bob over to Tartuga. I have no idea when Anderson will be back so we're just going to have to get ourselves there. Go." I say a silent prayer that we get over there before the storm hits.

I think about taking Luke and Annie with us, but I just know Jonah and Anderson wouldn't have left them here if they had gone far. They have their own rules about what they're supposed to do, just like Mike, PJ and I have ours. Besides, I feel like I can't risk anything happening to them on the boat. It's one thing for me to make this decision about my own brothers, but not Luke and Annie. They're better off on land.

I write a quick note to Jonah and Anderson, noting the time, 11:30 a.m., and telling them we've gone to Tartuga on Bob. Mike runs up ahead of us to Anderson's and tapes the note to his front door.

PJ and I make our way slowly to the dock, where Mike is waiting for us.

We set PJ below in a nest of blankets so he won't roll around.

"You okay?" I ask, afraid to hear him say no because there's just nothing I can do.

"Mmm-hmm," he says. He's looking a little drowsy and he's not trembling anymore. Maybe the pill is working. Okay. We can do this, I think. It's just a few miles.

On deck, Mike and I work together without talking. We both know what to do. I cross my fingers before I try starting the engine. *Assume it won't start*, I hear Sheryl's voice in my head. But it does start, on the first try. A good omen, I think. We're going to make it with no problem. I can do this.

We motor away from the dock and point the boat straight toward South Harbor.

We're only doing three knots with the motor going full blast. At this rate, it will take us forever. There are white-caps in the channel and it's getting really windy.

I keep looking around for rain, but it's still miles away.

"Mike, put on a life vest, okay? We're going to raise the main and motor sail so we'll get there faster."

"I'll raise it," he says.

"As soon as you get a life vest on. Check on PJ while you're down there."

Mike gives me a pained look. "I don't need a vest."

"Mike, *please*. Just put it on. I know you don't need one, but I'll feel a lot better. And I need your help, so hurry up." He doesn't move. "Besides," I say, "I need you. If you fall overboard and drown, what am I going to do?"

He's not buying it, but he goes below and comes back wearing an orange vest. He brings one for me, too and I put it on.

Mike raises the sail while I hold the boat. We pick up about two knots of speed. Much better. We might reach Tartuga in another forty-five minutes.

"How'd PJ look?" I say.

"Like he wants to cry, but he's not."

And then *wham*.

At first I don't know what it is. I think: earthquake, but that's ridiculous. It's just the only thing I know that is so sudden and so strong. The boat feels like it's been grabbed out of my hands and tossed over onto its side like a plastic toy.

For a minute I think we're going over and PJ's not wearing a life vest but the boat rights itself fast, then spins up into the wind. Then bam, we're heeled way over again. I can barely hold the tiller. I pull it all the way into my chest, trying to keep the boat straight, not wanting to look left or right and see that ocean come up at me again like blue-black outer space.

Okay, okay, I think. I can do this. *Just don't panic.*

"I'm *not* panicking," Mike says.

I stare at him. I must have been thinking out loud.

"I know," I say. "You're doing great." For a minute I think it's over, the wind is steady, blowing hard, but not gusting like it was. Then it hits us again, really hard. The boat bounces back, though. It's supposed to, I remind myself. There are tons of lead keel beneath us, making us pop back up every time. Right. Okay. Just think about that.

"Mike, hold the tiller. I'm going forward before we get another gust." I hold my voice really steady.

Where did this wind come from? I've never felt anything like it, it's like an enormous invisible wall that someone who's really, really angry is shoving our way.

I inch my way forward, clinging to things as I go, and when I'm at the mast, hugging it with both arms and my clenched knees, I shout to Mike to hold the boat steady, into the wind—even though it feels like the wind is everywhere—but he does it. No more gusts, just steady wind. Okay.

I release the halyard, hanging on tight, and let the main

drop a couple of feet. I have to yank the sail down the rest of the way with my left hand. I have one leg wrapped around the mast. I'm so afraid of being tossed into the water and leaving Mike and PJ alone on the boat.

When the second grommet passes through my hands, I hook it to the boom and tighten the halyard, then recleat it. The sail area has been reduced by about half, which will make it much easier to control the boat. I try tying up the extra sail that's hanging down, but I don't do a very good job. I'm not secure on deck so I just leave most of it flapping and crawl on my hands and knees back into the cockpit.

Rain. Of course, it had to come and here it is. We're completely drenched in seconds. I look across to Tartuga. There's so much chop in the channel that we've slowed way down. The rain is swallowing up Tartuga. I can barely see its outline. My heart sinks. There is no way. We're not going to make it. We'll be lucky if we get back to Ginger.

"Mike, this is impossible. We're going back."

"Right," Mike says.

I turn the boat around and start heading back. It's hard to see because of the rain in my eyes and the darkening sky. Behind us, Tartuga has been completely engulfed by the downpour. We would never have made it; I'm worried that by the time we reach Ginger, we won't be able to see it, either, and we'll just crash right into it.

The wind dies down a little as the rain increases. Mike drops the main the rest of the way for me and even manages to tie it up in kind of a bunchy mound on the boom. We motor back, the boat rising and falling over the swells like a carousel horse. When we reach the dock, Mike jumps off and ties the boat up. We rig two extra dock lines to help secure it.

Down below, PJ is asleep. It doesn't seem possible, but he's completely knocked out. The blankets worked, though; he didn't roll off the bunk. Mike and I rouse him and get him off the boat. It's not until I'm standing on the dock that my legs start to shake. Or maybe they were shaking all along and I just didn't notice.

We arrive a huddled, sopping mess at Anderson's door. I am afraid to leave Mike and PJ for even a second, so I make them come with me to get Luke and Annie. They look scared. The light outside is an ominous dark gray, as if someone moved the sun about a million light-years farther out into the universe. It's only one o'clock.

Jonah and Anderson still haven't come back. Where *are* they? It can't be safe out in the channel. The wind is blowing so hard now that big waves are crashing on the beach, just like at home. I tell Luke and Annie to get their rain gear, I'm taking them back to Dad's house. It's way too exposed here, we'll all be better off on the other side of the hill. Besides, I know we have a basement full of flashlights and water bottles.

Luke won't go down into their storeroom, where their foul-weather gear is hanging. "Uncle Anderson won't let us," he tells me. "There's no staircase, just a wooden ladder nailed to the wall. He says we might fall."

Mike volunteers and heads off. Five minutes later, he's still down there.

"Mike," I say, standing at the hatch in the floor that

opens into the storeroom. "Come on. What are you doing? We've got to get going."

"Casey," he says, softly, "can you come down here a second?" Something about the way he says it, I can tell he's not messing around. I grab the handhold at the top of the ladder and go down backward, the way you would into a swimming pool.

"What is it, Mike?"

"Look."

Turtle shells. A bunch of them. Even before it registers what they are, even before I start to think about what they're doing here, what this means, my breathing speeds up and my heart starts racing. I stand in front of a pile of them, stacked like bowls, and touch the edge of one lightly. I want to throw up.

I look around. There's a stained worktable, a basin, a bunch of different kinds of tools hanging on the wall and a wire trap like the kind we've seen snorkeling, the kind the islanders use to catch grouper and bass. This one is much bigger, though, big enough to hold a sea turtle.

"Okay, Mike. Not a word. Grab the jackets. Let's go."

Mike nods, makes a bundle out of the yellow rain jackets and follows me up the ladder.

Before we step back into the living room, I turn around to face Mike.

"I know," he says, and presses his lips together.

16

Both routes back to the house are treacherous. The beach would be worse, we decide. Because of the surf, we'd be up to our knees. It's not much better along the path. The wind is blowing so hard the trees are bent over, as if they're in gym class, doing side bends. Stuff is flying past us, branches and leaves. Even the rain feels like a solid object.

With all these short little kids in their yellow foul-weather gear trailing me I feel like I'm leading a parade of live fire hydrants through the woods.

There's a huge branch blocking the front door so we go in through the kitchen. Inside everything looks okay. No water coming in.

The electricity's off, though, and it's dark and muggy. Luckily the place is crawling with flashlights. We accidentally kick them over as we feel our way in the dark, and they roll around like bowling pins until we capture a few and light the place up. I send the kids into the basement and toss a few pillows and blankets down after them.

While Mike rounds up supplies, I raid the kitchen. I grab two loaves of bread, peanut butter, a knife, a bag of cookies, BBQ Pringles and the sack of oranges sitting on the kitchen counter.

"Hurry up, Mike," I call.

"Two minutes," he yells back to me from somewhere. The wind sounds like the freeway at rush hour. I can barely hear Mike, but I can see the beam of his flashlight bouncing around.

In the basement, I settle PJ into a canvas beach chair with a pillow to rest his arm on. It seems like the swelling's gone down, but I'm not really sure. He's pale, even through his tan.

Mike comes down a second later. He's got the handheld VHF and the first-aid kit.

Mike inspects PJ's bandages and loosens the sling around his neck. He looks at his watch. "It's not time for PJ's pill yet." Mr. Nursemaid.

We just sit there: PJ, Mike, Luke, Annie and me, staring at each other. There's nothing to do. I try to think of things to talk about, but all I can think of is the turtle shells in Anderson's workroom.

All the time he's been working for my dad, he's been poaching. He must have taken the two turtles that PJ saw were missing. The others he must have either killed before we got here and PJ started counting turtles, or he caught them once they were released. Or maybe he's trapping them out in the open sea, that's why there was a trap in the storeroom. He's always out somewhere in the Whaler.

And Jonah. Does he *know?* How can he *not* know? I think of him working all these mornings with my dad, setting up all those nets to protect the turtle hatchlings; rescuing that turtle that was stuck. The last time we were on Tartuga, he even fished a plastic bag out of the water in South Harbor so a turtle wouldn't mistake it for a jellyfish. I can't imagine him hurting the turtles.

But what about that awful scraping tool Jonah was using to pry barnacles off the Whaler? I know I saw the same tool hanging on the rack over the workbench in Anderson's storeroom. Unless there are two of them, that's where Jonah must have gotten it from. That means he's been in the storeroom before and he knew what was down there.

I really believed Jonah cared about the island ecology and the sea life, especially the turtles. And me. How could he care about me and still be doing such a hateful thing behind my father's back? Plus I don't understand why. It has to be for the money that the shells bring. But Dad's paying them both, I know that. I've heard, though, that people will pay a lot of money for those shells, since they're illegal. It makes me sick.

Mike's been poking around in boxes, and he comes up with a box that must be Dad's equivalent of the Rainy Day Fun Box my third-grade teacher used to pull out in bad weather. There's checkers, Old Maid, some jigsaw puzzles and a stack of paperback books. I look through them. *Great Tales & Poems of Edgar Allan Poe,* Stephen King's *The Shining, The Dark: New Ghost Stories,* Sebastian Junger's *The*

Perfect Storm. Jeez, I feel like the universe is having a little joke on me. It's spooky enough around here with the wind howling and the eerie flashlight beams. All we're missing is a radio report saying a crazed maniac has escaped from a local insane asylum. A crazed maniac with a hook for an arm. A hook and a speedboat.

I flip through more of the books until I find what I'm looking for: *The Notorious Jumping Frog of Calaveras County*. I read a couple of pages to myself. Worth a try. I figure I'll read to everybody, but when I look up everyone but Annie has nodded off. She's on the floor playing checkers with herself. She actually gets up and changes sides when it's the other side's turn.

"King me," she says to her opponent, changes sides and reluctantly tops off the checker that made it all the way across.

"Who won?" I ask her when she tips the board and slides the checkers back into their box.

"Me."

I stand on an overturned crate and try to look out the thin strip of windows that are a little above ground level. It's a complete blur outside, but it's not as dark as I expected. It's white, as if we're caught in a snowstorm instead of in a hurricane.

Is this a hurricane?

The squall that Jonah, PJ and I got caught in brought a lot of rain and wind, but it didn't last more than twenty minutes. This could still be over soon, I think. I hope.

An hour later, I wake up, surprised that I fell asleep. Now it's really blowing—screeching, really. The noise is incredible.

It's the loudest noise I've ever heard, like a hundred trains going a hundred miles an hour, right over our heads. Every now and then there's a huge noise, like a car wreck, and we all look up. The patio furniture, maybe, or tree branches. Who knows?

I make peanut butter roll-up sandwiches and pass them around.

On the radio we hear all kinds of distress calls from boats and a few weather reports. They say it's blowing ninety miles an hour. I try to imagine ninety-mile-an-hour wind.

"How hard do you think it was blowing when we were out in the channel, Mike?"

"Twenty-five knots," he says with confidence. "The Beaufort Scale says when there's whitecaps and ten-foot waves, which there were, it's blowing twenty-five knots, or about twenty-eight miles an hour. The gusts were more, maybe up to forty knots."

"Boy Scouts?" I say.

"Yeah." He grins. Then I giggle and so does he. Pretty soon we're laughing and Annie and Luke are too. We can't stop. After a while, we're just laughing at each other laughing. Somehow, PJ sleeps.

But then I'm crying. I can't help it. I don't want to cry and scare these guys. I'm so grateful that *they* haven't cried or even acted afraid but, suddenly, I just feel super-lonely even packed into this tiny basement with four other people. It's just that they are little kids and I have to be in charge. As angry as I feel at Jonah right now, I wish he were here with us. It would make me feel a lot better, although I'd have a few questions for him. I rest my head on my knees, so they won't see me cry.

Every time I wake up I'm surprised that I've been sleeping, and that everyone else is too. I'm imagining myself telling this story later and having to say, "Yeah, it was a *huge* storm. What did I do? Oh, I slept. And, oh yeah, I also ate a whole bag of Mother's Animal Cookies. Yeah, that's right, those pink-and-white frosted ones. All by myself."

Mike's shaking my arm, "Casey. Wake up. It's time."

"Time to go?" I say, taking a second to remember where we are and what's going on.

"No, for Dad to call."

Dad. I jump up and turn the radio on. We've only been turning it on for a few minutes at a time, to save the batteries.

"Are you going to tell him?" Mike says. We both know he's not talking about PJ's arm.

"Not now. When they get back, we'll tell him," I say. "Don't say anything to the kids, either."

"Well, I haven't, have I?"

"No. And thanks, Mike."

We tune in to Channel 22. We hear two people on Tartuga talking about trying to get some water and other supplies to the school, where some people have been put up for the night. They sound like they're shouting. At least we know the channel is working. I guess they're having a pretty bad time of it on the island. I guess we are too, from what it sounds like upstairs. But down here it's very still. Hot, even, which is probably why we've all been so drowsy and keep falling asleep.

Is Jonah out there in it? If he and Anderson had gotten back to the island safely, wouldn't they have come looking for us by now? They might be hurt. Or drowned. No, I tell myself, they must be stuck on Tartuga, maybe they're even with Jonah's mom and the twins.

No Dad. We listen hopefully until nine o'clock and then we turn off the radio. If Dad *could* have called, he *would* have by now. We have to save the batteries in case we need the radio later.

I turn off my thoughts when I click off the radio. I can't think about Sheryl and Dad and where they might be and why they couldn't call. I don't want to think about Jonah anymore. There just aren't enough possibilities. I've worked hard to come up with something, anything, that would make me feel sure he doesn't know what his uncle's been doing with the turtles—but how is that possible?

I pass around Pringles and oranges. Mike emptied the tool cabinet, and we stuck the portable toilet in there so we'd have privacy and now we're all ready to use it, taking a flashlight in there with us when it's our turn.

Three of the flashlights have died. The rest, which we've kept lit, standing on their ends, are starting to dim. We have four in reserve. I ask Luke and Mike to unfold the rest of the cots. Annie and I pick up all the stuff we've managed to spread around the floor: mostly games, books, food and our rain gear.

When everyone's settled, we click off the flashlights. Of course, now that we've been napping all day, no one can sleep. Also, the dark changes everything. Now it really is scary—*a dark and stormy night*. I turn one light back on and point it away from us, toward the wall. Like a night-light.

"I want you guys to know that I really appreciate how brave you've been. And cooperative," I say.

"We did this before," Annie says.

"Slept in the basement?" PJ asks. He still has a dopey sound. Mike's kept him medicated all day.

"In a storm like this one?" Mike asks.

"Worse," Luke says. "A lot worse than this. We had to sleep in the bathroom because it was the only room without windows. We didn't have a basement. Our roof blew off."

I just listen while he talks quietly about Hurricane Gabriel, three years ago. I have a feeling most of what he thinks he remembers he's actually been told, but it makes a good story. Everyone is really quiet listening and pretty soon I hear steady breathing and, one by one, all the brave little Indians nod off. I turn off our night-light and just lie there listening to the amazing racket outside. How can it still be blowing?

I'm still awake when the windows burst into the room. They don't break until they hit the concrete floor. It's an amazing sensation, first suction and then a blast of rain and wind. Everybody is up at once.

"Freeze!" I scream. "Nobody move!" I know there's broken glass everywhere. I feel for my tennies and shake them out before putting them on. I find a flashlight and sweep it over Mike, Annie, PJ and Luke.

I've heard these stories, that sometimes bodies in the morgue will sit up suddenly—some kind of weird muscle contraction. Well, that's how it looks down here, like I'm surrounded by corpses, frozen stiff, sitting up, their eyes wide open. But everyone is okay.

I can't believe no one was hit by a flying window. If anyone had been sitting up, they could have been decapitated. I can't even think about it.

I have to shout, but I get everyone to shake out their clothes, put their shoes on and get up against the wall underneath where the windows used to be. We're better protected here, although the rain is really shooting in. We make a mound of ourselves and use the foul-weather gear to top it all off. Poor PJ, I know he's in pain. He's right up against me and I can feel him whimpering, though I can't hear him because of the deafening roar of the wind over our heads.

On the bright side . . . it's a lot less stuffy in here.

17

When morning comes, we're still a confused heap of wet bodies. We can tell it's morning because there's light, finally, and we can see the light because the hurricane has passed. We don't move right away. We probably sit there for ten minutes, afraid it's just a lull. But it really is over.

After we untangle ourselves and look around, we can't believe our eyes. The entire basement, floor and walls, is covered—covered—with leaves. There isn't one square inch of surface that isn't completely plastered with leaves. It's like some kind of strange environmental wallpaper.

Mike climbs on the crate and looks out the window holes. "All clear!" he says. We cheer and holler and the basement door suddenly flies open.

Jonah stares down at us. "What are *you* guys doing here?"

Annie and Luke both run to him.

When I stand up, I feel like my bones are made of

rubber. Apparently my voice is made of thin air because even though I open my mouth, nothing happens.

Mike says, "This was the safest place. Where'd you expect us to be?"

"On Tartuga," Jonah says. "That's what your note said. I thought you spent the whole night over there. I figured you were with my mom and the twins."

The note Mike pinned to their front door! When was that? Yesterday, a hundred years ago, when it was just raining and it was only eleven-thirty and PJ had just fallen.

"I just came over to make sure your dad's place was okay and to get the handheld VHF when I heard you guys yelling. Wow," Jonah says, looking past us at the mess in the basement and taking in the broken windows. "I'm really glad to see you all. And really surprised."

"Jonah," I say, "PJ's hurt his arm. It might be broken. We need to get him over to the clinic. Is the Whaler here?"

Jonah tells us he left Anderson on Tartuga late yesterday afternoon and came back to the island alone, thinking he'd square things away before the storm and ride it out with us. Since the Whaler can do twenty knots, he was able to make the channel crossing without too much trouble, cutting through the swells. He got back to the island about the time we were all huddling in Dad's basement. When he saw the note we left, he just assumed I'd taken Luke and Annie, as well as Mike and PJ, to Tartuga.

He's been explaining all this as we pick up our stuff and clear out of the basement. I've hardly been able to look at him, though, because I feel so betrayed. And it seems to me that Jonah is talking a little faster than usual, and not look-ing at me, either. I can't tell if he knows what I'm thinking or if he's just keyed up because of the storm or if he's figured out that I must have found out about what's in his storeroom since I have Luke and Annie with me and they have their foul-weather gear with them.

Whatever it is, the awkward atmosphere around here is as thick as the humidity, which seems to have doubled from its usual million percent since the wind stopped blowing.

But I can't think about any of this right now. The most important thing now is to get PJ to the clinic and I need Jonah for that. I can worry about the rest later.

Since all six of us won't fit in the Whaler, I leave Mike behind with Luke and Annie and a bunch of instructions not to let them out of his sight and not to go digging around in any wreckage and to stay out of the water and . . . and fi-nally Mike gives me a pleading look and I say, "Okay, I'm sorry. I know you'll be responsible, Mike. Really, I appreciate all your help with PJ and the boat and everything. But just be smart, okay?"

I know he will be. In fact, I feel better leaving the kids with Mike than I would with Anderson.

After everything PJ's had to do on his own in the last twenty hours, it's almost silly that Jonah carries him all the way to the Whaler. But it's nice for PJ and it's nice of Jonah. Jonah feels terrible, and he can't stop apologizing for not know-ing we were here on the island all along, and for not being with us during the storm.

"Even though I forgot to take the note down, didn't you

realize we were here when you saw Bob at the dock?" I say, finally. It's about the first thing I've said to him since we packed up PJ and left our house.

"Bob isn't here, Casey," Jonah says. We all look toward the dock. Not only is Bob not there, the whole dock is gone. All that's left are the pilings sticking up out of the water. I guess we did a good job of tying Bob to the dock. Too bad we couldn't tie the dock up to the island. Poor Dad. He loves that boat.

The whole island is a mess. The landscape looks like an enormous version of my bedroom after I've been digging through my closet looking for something to wear. Trees have been tossed, literally, all over the place. The air smells like fresh-cut wood. Not one of the trees still standing has a single leaf left on it.

The sea is a murky brown. There are branches and furniture and huge pieces of wood floating at the shoreline. None of the furniture is ours. It must have washed over from Tartuga. Our patio chairs are piled up against the side of the house.

It's hard to keep my mouth from hanging open as we make our way through the mess and to the dock in front of Anderson's place. His house is gone. I gasp when I see it and Jonah nods.

"You did the right thing, taking everybody down into your basement."

The house has been completely blown away, right down to the foundation. The roof, one piece of corrugated tin, is lying on the beach, one sharp corner of it dug into the sand. There are clothes and papers and *things* everywhere. This is what a bombing looks like, I think.

"Where were you during all this?" I say, finally.

"In our storeroom, just like you guys."

And there's my answer. He knows; he's been sitting in there with a stack of turtle shells all night.

"By the time I got back on the island, it was too late to even get over to your place. I knew Paul had supplies and stuff, but there was no way I could make it even that far. Trees were being uprooted, and I just barely made it into our own storeroom before the roof blew off. The rest of the house went around three this morning."

That's about the time the windows blew in on us.

"Could you tell when the roof went?" I ask, not ready, yet, to ask him the only thing I really want to know.

"I heard things slamming around but it was hard to tell what was going on. I was shocked this morning, but I guess I wasn't surprised. You were lucky because you're protected by the hillside."

"Yeah," I say. "Do you know if your place on Tartuga is okay?"

"No, I haven't reached my mom. That's why I was looking for the radio. I hope she was evacuated to the school. We can find out when we get over there."

He puts PJ in the bottom of the Whaler and wedges blankets around him to support him.

As we head away from the island, I look back and see Mike and Annie and Luke milling around the wreckage in front of our house. Wait till they see Anderson's place, I think. Mike will flip. Mr. Serious in a Storm.

"Jonah," PJ says from his nest of blankets. "Are the turtles okay? Were they trapped by the storm?"

"They're fine," Jonah says, giving me the wheel so he can kneel down next to PJ and talk to him.

"The first thing I did when the storm was over," Jonah says to PJ, "was go down to the beach and make sure that nothing had happened to them. They've probably lived through lots of storms like this before. They're older than you and me put together, and this is *my* third hurricane."

PJ smiles. "Good," he says, "I was thinking about them all night. I was afraid their pen would break up and they'd get tangled in the nets."

"Nope. I knew you would be worried, but they're really fine," Jonah says. "Honest." He smiles up at me.

I can barely look at Jonah. He's being so nice to me, and to PJ, but I feel like it's all fake, that underneath he's a liar, a *turtle killer*.

"Of course," Jonah says, taking his seat again at the wheel, "if I'd known you were still on the island I would have come to your place first. I would probably have headed right over to Tartuga after looking in on your place if I hadn't heard you guys shouting. I was so happy to see you." He slips his arm across my back and squeezes my shoulder. I move away by turning in my seat and pretending to adjust the blankets around PJ. When I turn back toward the front of the boat, my foot kicks something that clangs against the floorboards. I reach down and pull up the tool Jonah was using to pry barnacles off the Whaler that day we took it to Tartuga. My heart leaps against my ribs: so there is another tool just like the one I saw in the basement. Maybe this tool is always in the Whaler and Jonah didn't get it out of the storeroom after all. Maybe he didn't know about the turtles any sooner than I did, or at least not before spending last night down there. But then why hasn't he said anything?

At the clinic they take PJ into X-ray. We talk to some people and find out Jonah's mom and the twins are indeed at the school as Jonah thought. He asks someone he knows who is going over to the school with cases of water to let his mom know where he is and that he's okay.

He and I wait outside on the steps. It's way too crowded inside the clinic. There's no word about Dad and Sheryl. So far we've heard about a lot of property damage on this and the other islands in the storm's path, but not about any injuries. The way news is traveling from person to person, I feel pretty sure that if anything had happened to them, someone on Tartuga would have heard about it by now. And even if they don't know me, everyone in town knows Jonah and that he's been working on Ginger with my dad. There are lots of people in the street, trading stories, just like at home after an earthquake.

"This is really something, isn't it?" Jonah says.

We're sitting so close together that our shoulders, arms and legs are touching. I want to move away and yet I don't want to move. He feels good next to me, but I'm so angry that I want to punch him hard or hug him and have him say *I just found out the most awful thing about my uncle*.

But I can't stand this weird silence anymore, and I can't stand not knowing.

"Jonah," I say, "I know about the turtles. I was in your storeroom. I saw the shells."

I feel all his muscles tense against me, so much so that

he's shrunk and without moving he's no longer touching me anywhere. I wait, but he doesn't say a word.

"Jonah?"

"I'm sorry you had to see those, Casey. PJ didn't see them, did he?"

"No, just me and Mike," I say. And then, "Jonah, did you kill those turtles?"

He stares at me. "Do you *think* that? Do you actually think I could do that?"

"I would never have thought so, but then we saw the shells, and you must have known."

Jonah reaches for me, but I shove him away.

"Casey, Casey, wait a minute. I could *never* do that. In fact, I can't believe you would ever think I'd *poach* turtles." I think I hear a catch in his voice. Or maybe I just *want* to hear a catch. I can't read his face at all. He looks really serious.

"Well, I didn't know what to think," I say.

"You could have asked."

"That's what I'm doing now," I say, realizing he's right. I haven't given him a chance to explain.

"Day before yesterday, when I took my mom and the twins home, I noticed there were two turtles missing. I wanted to find Anderson and tell him. He wasn't in his workroom, but the hatch was open and that's when I saw the shells. I'd never been in there before; it's usually locked. Until that moment I had no idea what was going on."

PJ had told me there were two missing. When was that? *Yesterday*. Just before everything happened. That's why he climbed the tree, so he could get a better view of the beach and find the missing turtles.

"My head was spinning. All I could think of was how this must have been going on right under my nose. How all summer I've been there working with your dad and my uncle and I never once noticed anything unusual. Then I realized that I *have* been kind of preoccupied." He looks at me pointedly and raises his eyebrow. "I kept trying to come up with reasons for why what I was seeing couldn't be what it looked like. I really wanted there to be a good explanation. Finally I realized there probably just wasn't, and I was going to have to talk to Anderson."

"So did you?"

"I tagged along with him yesterday when he left the island. I felt like I had to talk to him before I told your dad."

"So you were going to tell my dad?"

"Of course, Casey," Jonah says, giving me a strange look. "I was hoping there was some explanation, any explanation, although I couldn't imagine what it would be. But I wanted to at least give Anderson a chance to explain," he says.

"Okay, I get your point."

"Course," Jonah says, "there wasn't much to think except the obvious. I mean, I knew it was Anderson. It couldn't have been your dad. It wasn't me, and there's no one else. I wanted to bring it up the minute we got in the Whaler and away from the island, but it took me all the way to Tartuga to get the words out of my mouth." He lets out a long breath, then looks at me. He looks so sad—then he kind of puts his fingers together at the center of his forehead and draws them apart, across his eyebrows to his temples. It's a gesture I've seen my dad do a thousand times and I wonder if that's where Jonah picked it up.

"Anyway, after I confronted him we got in a big fight. That's why I was gone so long. I would have sent Luke and Annie over to your place if I'd known how things were going to turn out. Needless to say, he decided not to come back to Ginger with me and face your dad. You've gotta believe me, Casey. I was as shocked as you are. And, believe me, I'm just as upset."

"I do believe you."

"I'm really so sorry, Casey. If only I'd found out sooner, I could have saved at least *some* turtles." When he says this last part I'm *sure* I hear a catch in his voice.

"I know," I say. Jonah pulls me toward him and wraps his arms around me tight. And then my tears just come. I cry and cry. It's not just the turtles; it's everything: the hurricane, the mess, PJ, and it's my relief that the terrible things I imagined about Jonah aren't true, weren't even possible.

The doctor tells us that PJ's fracture is not serious and that his arm just needs to be rewrapped up. We'll be able to take him home in a little while.

"Are you going to tell PJ?" Jonah asks when we're back outside.

"I don't know," I say. "I feel like I should wait for Dad and see what he says, but then I have no idea where he and Sheryl are, or when we'll see them."

"I have a feeling it'll be sooner than you think," Jonah says, looking past me to the water. He puts his hands on

my shoulders and spins me around. There they are, Dad and
Sheryl, waiting to get off the ferry that's just docking. God,
I'm so relieved to see them.

"Let's go tell him right now," Jonah says.

"No, let's wait till after he sees PJ," I say.

"Sure," Jonah says, and takes my hand. We run across
the road and meet Dad and Sheryl as they step off the boat.

18

Dad and Sheryl go into the clinic to see PJ and talk to the doctor. It's going to be another hour until PJ is released and Dad is anxious to get back to Ginger and see the damage, plus he doesn't want to leave the kids there too much longer, so Jonah and I will wait here for PJ. Dad and Sheryl will take a water taxi over. All their equipment won't fit in the taxi, so Jonah and I pack it into the Whaler. While we're stowing their gear, we decide to break the news about Bob to Dad. He's going to see that the dock is gone as soon as he gets to Ginger.

Sheryl seems more upset about Bob than Dad does. He's been taking in all the hurricane damage here on Tartuga and, he tells us, they passed quite a bit of wreckage, including sailboats that were run aground, on their way up from St. George, so he kind of anticipated that Bob might not have made it through the hurricane.

"I doubt you could have done anything to save Bob,

Casey. I think you handled yourself well; I'm very proud of you. The important thing is that you all came through the night in one piece."

"Except PJ," I say.

"PJ will be just fine," Dad says, pulling me in for a one-armed hug. He has Sheryl under the other arm. She winks at me.

Dad and Jonah head over to the dock to make arrangements with the water taxi service. I tell Sheryl that her and Dad's house is a mess, but not damaged. I tell her Anderson's house was completely destroyed. I feel as if I have to get all this stuff out fast, before they find out on their own. I don't want them to be too shocked when they get over there. They'll still have one awful surprise waiting for them. I'm wondering if I should tell her about Anderson and the turtles right now, even though I told Jonah we could wait until tomorrow to tell Dad, but then I see Dad and Jonah crossing the road toward us.

Sheryl gives me a kiss on the cheek and says, "I want you to know that I think you were very brave to try to bring PJ over in Bob, and you were smart to turn back when you did. I knew you would make a good sailor."

"Because of you," I say, and give her a wink of my own, then a hug.

When Dad and Jonah reach us I can tell Dad is really upset.

"I told him about Anderson, Casey," Jonah says to me. "I'm sorry, I know we said we'd wait, but I just wanted to get it over with."

"That's okay," I say. "I was thinking the same thing."

Sheryl looks from Dad to Jonah and back to Dad. "What's going on?"

"Apparently," Dad says, clearing his throat, "our very own Anderson has been poaching turtles. Probably from out in the sea, but also from our own pens at White Bay."

Sheryl lets out a little gasp and brings her hand up to her mouth. She looks at Jonah and he nods at her. He looks kind of helpless right then, like he'd like to take back what Dad just said. His face and neck flush red and for an awful minute I think he's going to cry. He kind of waves his hands in the air as if he wants to explain but he just can't and he drops his hands to his sides as if to say, "There's nothing I can say."

Sheryl grabs my dad's arm with one hand and Jonah's with the other. To my dad she says, "Oh, Paul, I'm so sorry, you must really feel betrayed." Then she turns to Jonah and says, "And this must be awful for you, Jonah; I know the turtle project has meant as much to you as it has to Paul and I'm sure you're mortified at what Anderson has done."

Wow, I think. She's pretty cool. In about ten seconds she's covered everything and I can see by looking at Jonah that she's made him feel much better. I hadn't even thought of it, but he must have thought that my dad and Sheryl would hold all this against him because he's Anderson's nephew. Obviously Sheryl understood all that immediately.

She leans into Dad and says something we can't hear, then puts her arms around him. They stand that way for a long minute; then Dad walks off toward a policeman standing in front of the clinic.

Jonah says, "Your dad said he wants to stay here and file a report. He'll wait for PJ and bring him back. I'll take you and Sheryl over to Ginger now, then bring Luke and Annie back here so we can stay at my mom's." Right. For a minute I'd forgotten that Anderson's house on Ginger is gone.

"You poor things," Sheryl says. "You've had an even worse time than we'd imagined. And I'm so sorry for PJ— I know he loves those turtles."

"We haven't told him," I tell her. "I thought I'd let Dad decide about that."

"That's probably a good idea," she says.

Nobody can sign PJ's cast because he doesn't get one. He gets a blue canvas sling with white trim and he's excused from the disaster cleanup crew, which is me, Mike, Dad, Sheryl and Jonah.

The clinic didn't do a much better job of wrapping up PJ's arm than Mike did. I make sure to point this out to Mike. He's quite pleased.

Jonah's house on Tartuga lost its roof. Mary and the twins spent the night of the hurricane at the school. They went back to their house the next day. Since their roof came off in one piece, the neighbors all got together and helped them put it back on. All the roofs on Tartuga are just giant sheets of corrugated tin. There were lots of them lying around after the storm. It makes me shudder to think of how dangerous it would have been to be out during the storm with all these roofs slicing through the air.

Everyone was a little worried that Anderson might

disappear, but he spent the first night after the hurricane at Jonah's mom's. Jonah said he didn't come in until after everyone had gone to bed, probably so he wouldn't have to face them. Jonah said he was glad of that because he was still too angry to talk to him and he didn't want to look at his face. The police came in the morning and arrested him. He didn't try to deny anything, he just listened to the charges and then walked out to the police car with his head hanging and got in the backseat. No handcuffs or anything. I could tell that it must have been awful for Jonah and that even though he's disgusted with Anderson, he feels sorry for him. He said the whole thing was humiliating and that he was embarrassed for his uncle and for himself. He keeps apologizing to my dad, even though it wasn't his fault and Dad has told him that a hundred times.

There will be a hearing and Anderson might go to jail. Dad said he'd call us in California and let us know as soon as anything happens.

We've spent the last couple of days trying to clean up around the island. The first day we hauled all kinds of stuff out of the water. The water is all murky and churned up. Even with our masks on, it's hard to see more than a few feet underwater. Lots of debris washed up along the shore. Most of it is from Anderson's house, but some of it must have blown all the way over here from Tartuga. We made a pile of it to take over there in case anyone is looking for it. Mostly it's clothes, but we also found things like a teakettle, toys, even a radio. I keep thinking of us all squared away in the basement while all this stuff was catapulting around over our heads.

This morning we boarded up the windows in the basement and cleaned up the terrace and put all the patio furniture back. Things are starting to look a little bit normal, except for the trees not having any leaves, which is really strange.

Jonah and Dad have been hauling branches and giant palms fronds and piling them near the dock that survived at Turtle Bay.

Yesterday two fisherman from Tartuga showed up towing Bob behind their boat. They found him washed up on shore on a little cay five miles east of here. The rudder was broken and he'd been dismasted. The dinghy was gone. Dad said those things will be easy to fix. He was so happy to see Bob, he actually kissed one of the fishermen. I had a feeling Dad was more upset about losing Bob than he let on when we told him. The fishermen could have charged Dad for salvaging Bob, but they didn't. Everybody has been helping everybody else out.

The two missing turtles are dead, of course. We decided to tell PJ they were let out. What's the point in telling him the truth? He's been feeling bad enough as it is; he feels guilty because he hasn't spent much time this last week "talking to Coco in his head," as he puts it. There were a few things going on, I told him, like a fractured arm and a major hurricane to distract him from thinking about home. The same goes for me, but I've been thinking about home a lot more these past few days since we'll be leaving next week.

Jonah starts school in two days, so today is the last day I'll see him.

"I hate to leave the island when it looks like this," I tell him. "It's not exactly the picture I'd hoped to take home with me."

"I think you've got plenty of others," he says, grinning at me. He knows I took sixteen rolls of film before Cindy ripped through here, but I think he means the thousands of pictures in my head.

We're standing on the dock next to the Whaler. Dad's going to be down here any second to take Jonah over to Tartuga. I feel like everything's going too fast. I wish we had just one more day to go swimming, maybe sailing. But I've wished that every day this week.

There's just no getting around *the last time*. One way or another, it has to happen. Unless I just stayed here forever. Except I think Mom would be a little upset if I didn't turn up for school in September. And Jen.

And Matt, I hope.

I feel about them the way PJ feels about Coco. I haven't been "talking to them in my head" very much lately. They've just seemed so far away.

"The picture I want to have of *you*," Jonah says, "is swimming at Spring Bay in the moonlight. That's what I'll be thinking about."

"I think I'll picture you in the dinghy with your face in a plastic Clorox bottle, that day we went to Lizard Island," I say, laughing.

"No, you won't," he says. "You'll think about that same night and the full moon and standing out here in the pouring rain laughing with me."

"You're right," I say, "I will." And then Jonah takes my face in his hands and presses his lips to my forehead. He holds me like that for a long minute and then turns around without saying another word and heads down the path toward the dock.

Heading back to the house, I come upon a big fat green lizard sunning himself on the path. He doesn't budge. We eye each other for a moment, but when I start to step over him he runs away.

"Ha," I say, and keep going.

Lesley Dahl lives in Pasadena, California, with her husband and her dog, Ripley. She loves to sail, swim, and scuba dive, especially in warm Caribbean waters. At home she and Ripley spend most mornings hiking in the nearby mountains with their friends. She has always wanted to write books that kids would read, and this is her first one.